MINX

MAGGIE ADAMS

Cover Design by: Backcover KLPS

Editing: Maria Vickers

Formatting: Maria Vickers

CONTENTS

MINX

This book is dedicated to every woman who has fallen and then gotten back up.

Prologue

Hi! I'm Miranda Blake, and this is my story. Well, sort of. It's more like a twisted fairytale–if you believe in them–except there's no beautiful, young princess with perky breasts, perfectly coiffed hair, and a sassy attitude. I'm closing in on fifty, thirty pounds overweight, according to Weight Watchers, and after nursing two kids and that bitch gravity doing her job, I'm lucky the ladies don't hit my knees. The gorgeous brown mane of hair is slightly frizzy from my ridiculous attempts to recapture my youth by dyeing the hell out of it. As for my sassy attitude, well, it wasn't so long ago that I was a doormat. And the charming prince who swept me off my feet into the life of my dreams? I have a dog named Prince, German Shepherd, who knocks me on my ass if I'm in the way when the doorbell rings. Did that count?

In fairytales, the princess was usually helped by giving, compassionate companions of the animal variety for some reason. You would never see me anywhere near raccoons, squirrels, or–shudders–birds. I'd seen the movies. I knew the death tolls. Actually, no, I wasn't like them because I had friends, not minions to do my bidding. The kind that believed if life gave you lemons...well, you've heard the saying. Although, one of them would make a lovely lemon pound cake served with the appropriate tea and a dollop of exquisite whipped cream. While another would grab the tequila and salt and make margaritas. Yet another would slice the lemons right open, squirt her enemies in the eye as she growled and screamed, "Die, motherfucker!" And finally, my peace-loving friend would make cannabis lemon bars and pass them around with a smile while a hint of patchouli clung to her caftan. I'd simply add them to my water to counter any vitamin C deficiency and continue with my day.

Now, fairytales, folklore, and the occasional urban legend notwithstanding, my life was pretty ordinary, but wasn't that how these stories start out?

Once upon a time...

Chapter One

"I want a divorce."

I paused and looked up from packing our suitcases for our anniversary trip to Aruba. The ambient light he had insisted upon when we remodeled barely illuminated his form much less his facial expression. I didn't mind the lighting usually, it smoothed over the slight imperfections on our bodies and made everything appear more soft and supple. Tonight, I would have given my left boob for one of those interrogation lights you see on detective shows.

"I'm sorry. What did you say?" Like the doormat I was, I continued to fold his underwear and place it into the case. The frustration coming from his voice was enough to convince me he spoke the truth, but I didn't want to believe him. So, I continued to mess with the damn clothes like an idiot, hoping this was his idea of a twisted joke at my expense. I'd had a lot of those over the years.

"You heard me, Miranda." My husband, Daniel Blake, raked his right hand through his graying hair. For a moment, I felt a twinge of envy. Men were so damn lucky as they grew older. The gray and glasses made them appear sophisticated and worldly. I, however, looked like that myopic frizzy-haired witch in those wizard movies.

I blinked, returning his frown with a slight smile. "You don't mean that," I retorted, shaking my head. I could feel the panic beginning to rise. What if he did mean it? What would I do? I'd given up my job as a bookkeeper over twenty-five years ago to get married and have children. I'd stayed home and become the perfect housewife and mother because that was the way he wanted it. Anger began to replace the panic. I'd given up *my dreams* to allow him his, and this is how he repays me?

The clothes were packed so I started to move toward the bathroom to fill the toiletries. Brushing past him, I was surprised when he grabbed my arm. "You're not listening! God, you do this every time there's something you don't want to hear. Do you know how annoying that is?"

Annoying? Avoiding confrontation was annoying?? I almost laughed out loud. If he only knew how many times I had to choke down my screams, to swallow the demands, insisting he listen to me for once. Perhaps I should let fly right now and really allow the bastard to have it. After all, he deserved it with this stupid revelation.

Who the hell gets divorced after twenty-five years? I mean, that was like the last year to make a change, wasn't it?

After that, you take stock of your life, decide it may not be all you dreamed of, but it's good enough, and you wait each other out on the death sentence.

I opened my mouth to tell him just that when I noticed he moved away and was rifling through the suitcase. "What in the hell are you doing?" I growled at him and began refolding my things. "We are going on our anniversary cruise tomorrow morning. I need to pack. You need to get a grip on whatever this male menopause thing is and be ready to enjoy our trip."

Oh my God! Did I just say that out loud? I peeked up at him. His mouth opened and closed like a fish out of water. I watched the blood rush upward from his shirt, past his throat, to his head. Yep, I'd said it out loud.

He grabbed my arms and pushed me into the desk chair. I was suddenly frightened. *How odd!* I'd never been scared of him before. Perhaps it was because he pressed his face was so close to me that I could smell the whiskey on his breath and see myself in his eyes. But more than likely, it was because he had his fingers around my throat, and he was squeezing.

"Pay attention, Miranda. I no longer want you. I no longer desire you. You have become an albatross weighing me down. We are divorcing, and that's final. You go your way, and I go mine. I take what is mine, and you take what is yours." He released me and stepped back to the suitcase, calmly taking out my clothes once again.

"The kids?" I gasped out, rubbing the sting from the skin of my throat. Justin, twenty-one, and Jennifer, nineteen, were away at college.

"The kids are adults. They will be fine." He closed the suitcase with a snap. "I'm going on the cruise. When I return, I expect you to be out of the house. Everything can be handled through our lawyers."

The cruise. My clothes. His silences. I closed my eyes against the knowledge of my own stupidity. "Who is she?"

I could feel his stare. He was weighing whether to tell me or not, so it must be someone I knew. "It doesn't matter."

I opened my eyes. "It does to me."

For the first time, he seemed uneasy. Clearing his throat, he finally conceded, "It's Megan Clark. As soon as our divorce is final, she'll be Megan Blake."

"Our daughter's tennis coach?!" I shot up from the chair. "You've been fucking our daughter's tennis coach?!" This threw my fury into high gear like nothing else could. He could mess with me all he wanted, but to deliberately hurt our daughter, to use her for his selfish desires?

I shoved him out the bedroom door. "You cheating, sack of shit! You find my avoidance of issues *annoying*, well, let me help you clear the air! I find your constant handling of your balls *annoying*, your clearing your throat then swallowing phlegm *annoying*, your constant critique of everyone else *annoying*, your pompous attitude about my friends *annoying*!" I took a deep breath, noting with satisfaction he now clutched the suitcase to his chest in defense, and screamed at the top of my lungs, "But mostly, I find your selfish, narcissistic, cloying attempts to be the man you need to be but fall far short of to be *annoying!*"

"You're insane!" he whispered, horrified at my display.

He scrambled down the stairs and headed for the garage as I continued to hail insults down upon his head. "You're a terrible father to do this to your children! Your homemade wine tastes like raspberry piss water! Your mother's potato salad sucked!"

I saved the best for last. One that would ultimately worm its way into his psyche and take root. One this narcissistic rat bastard couldn't help but take to heart. The one thing I had to constantly praise him on. I smiled as he hurried into the car. "You're a mediocre fuck, Daniel. You're a one trick pony in bed and your balls smell like vegetable soup!" I made sure to imprint the expression of horror and disgust on his face as he backed out of our garage to rush to his lover.

It was only hours later, as I slid onto the sheets of the bed in the guestroom, that I realized throughout the entire confrontation, neither of us ever mentioned love. That made me sad for a moment, then a profound relief took hold, and I began to cry. I hadn't realized how tightly I had been wound. Fuckin' twenty-five years and I finally get a do-over.

Sliding my eyes shut, I dreamed.

I slept like the dead and woke to find the sun high in the sky and my entire body ached. My mouth was dry, my back and legs hurt, and my throat felt like I swallowed glass. I rolled out of bed knowing I was still in the clothes I had worn last night. That was the moment the memories of the argument and betrayal come flooding back, but I pushed them aside in order to get a drink of water and maybe a good shower.

I emerged from my ablutions feeling refreshed, if not happy, about my current situation. Wrapping a towel around myself, I reached for the blow dryer but stopped. A noise coming from the bedroom startled me. It sounded as if someone had bumped into the hope chest at the end of the bed.

Quietly, I unwound the cord from the dryer, prepared to bash my asshole husband with the business end of my Conair Super Max 1500. After all, it had to be him. Everyone else thought we were on our way to Aruba.

The bathroom door opened suddenly. I let out a shriek and swung the dryer, clashing with the object in my friend, Kimy's, hand. Her gun went off, burying a bullet into the side of my whirlpool tub, sending water sloshing all over my naked feet and the floor.

"What the fuck?" Kimy jumped to avoid the expanding puddle racing toward her. "Miranda, what the hell are you doing here? You're on your anniversary trip!"

I grabbed my towel, now soaked at my feet to cover my nakedness, which I realize dropping it was stupid in the first place, but I was just shot at by one of my best friends. I wasn't thinking clearly. "Me?" I screeched, "What are you doing in my house?"

In true Kimy style, she smirked. "I'm looking at a drowned poodle." She threw me a dry towel and slipped off her shoes. Wading through the mess, she calmly plugged the hole in the tub with the end of a wet washcloth and began cleaning up while I exchanged the wet towel for a dry one. "Get dressed and tell me why you're still here. I came by to check that you hadn't forgotten to activate your security code."

Kimy, my gun-toting, black-haired, goth-loving friend, was all about security. She'd been carjacked as a college student, driven to a remote area where the two idiots who had done the deed stopped to get high. She managed to escape easily since they were too stoned to see straight. Since then, she'd taken it upon herself to ensure that those she cared about were always alert and prepared. Thanks to her, I knew self-defense, how to fire a gun, and several useful household items to maim or kill an intruder. Next month, I was taking some sort of Krav Maga course. She promised ice cream after each session, so I was game.

After dressing, I sat on the bed, brushing out the tangles in my hair. She came in and plopped down beside me. "What happened?"

That was it. That was all she said, but it was that tone of soft compassion so rarely heard in my no-nonsense friend which was my undoing. The tears flowed and the words came out in a jumbled mess. At least, I was pretty certain they were nothing more than unintelligible blubbering because I couldn't even remember what I told her. She got the gist of it…I thought because the bed moved, and I heard her on the phone. When she finished, she was back and had me lie me down in the bed as she tucked me in and held me.

At some point, I slept, waking in the late evening to find Tessa, her honey blonde hair perfectly coiffed, as usual, sitting on the floor next to my bed. She was drinking tea in a cup from my wedding china while perusing Traditional

Home online. Sadie was lighting a bundle of what smelled like burnt socks and lavender, her bracelets jangling softly as she waved it around the room in time to something she was humming, her red curls danced in rhythm to her sways. Chloe and Kimy were drinking Coronas, chatting at the end of the bed. Chloe's platinum bob and Kimy's black chop reminded me of that *Ebony and Ivory* song.

Their goddess vibes, that was what we called the feelings we had for each other, seemed to reach me. You know, the kind of connection where you simply clicked with another person? Well, everything hit all at once because suddenly four pairs of eyes turned to me instantaneously. Tessa, the closest to me, kissed my hand while Chloe helped me sit up, Kimy fired questions at me, and Sadie, bless her, waved that smoking thingy all around me.

"How are you? Do you know where the bastard went? Should I call the school and let them know about that bitch coach? Have you told the children? Do you have a headache?"

"Kimy," Tessa intervened, stopping the interrogation with her firm but subtle command. She turned to me. "Do you need anything, honey?"

"I need to pee."

It was exactly the right thing to say to ease their worry. Smiles, then giggles broke out. I was helped out of bed with reminders to take it slow, my bladder wasn't what it used to be thanks to childbirth, and general crude comments you could only make to your very best buddies.

I slammed the door in their faces, which caused more

laughter and comments about bladder leakage and the urine evacuation scene from some *Austin Powers* movie.

It was in that moment, sitting on the toilet "evacuating", I realized I truly wasn't alone. Oh sure, I was terrified. I mean I went from my parent's home to marriage and children, now this. I washed my hands and peered into the mirror. Of course, I saw a few wrinkles. Continuing the perusal of my body, my stare drifting downward–OK, that could use some improvement. My inspection moved back up to my eyes. Bloodshot and puffy, but still a pretty green. Nothing some eye drops and a cold compress couldn't handle.

My ears picked up the chatter beyond the door, and my nose wrinkled at the foul smell Sadie had waved all over the other room. Yeah, I needed to deal with the stench right away. But that aside, my heart wasn't really broken, just bruised, and time would heal it, too. My soul, well, it was still as good as ever, and it would remain that way, thanks to those menopausal crazy, smelly, sometimes violent, but always compassionate friends on the other side of that door.

I grabbed my hairbrush before I started crying again since it would distract me momentarily. I brushed my hair, pulled it up in a ponytail, noting with a frown that the grays were showing up again. I wonder if I could still afford the salon. Maybe I should try one of those at-home kits. Shaking my head at my errant thoughts–maybe it was time for some focus supplements–I brought my mind back to business. Time to figure out what the hell to do with the rest of my life.

I opened the door with a deep breath and announced, "Goodbye, doormat!"

Everyone cheered.

Sadie shouted, "Hello…" her smile faded as if she didn't know what to say next.

Kimy shot her a dirty look and raised her beer. "Hello, badass babe!"

"Uh, no." Chloe studied me for a moment. "She's more a lady than a babe." They all stared at me, and I began to feel uncomfortable. "But not really a lady," Cloe mumbled.

All heads whipped around to look at Tessa.

"Um…" As she tried to think of what to say, I fidgeted in the doorway, and Tessa finally took pity on me. Putting her arms around me, she led me to the mirror, standing behind me. "We are all correct." She squeezed my shoulders. "You are a badass when you need to be. You brought down an armed intruder, naked, with a blow dryer." She winked at me. "And you are a lady–sociable, sweet, and graceful." I couldn't help but laugh. Everyone knew I was a klutz. She continued, "You are definitely not a doormat. You care, and you are one of the most compassionate people I have ever had the honor to call a friend. But in caring for everyone, you've lost yourself."

"But we know the real you, Miranda. You've been your true self with us." Chloe squeezed my hand, peering into the mirror.

"You're funny, sexy, and adventurous," Kimy stated, kissing me on top of my head.

Sadie came up on the other side of Tessa. "And you're tolerant and open to new ideas and friends."

I couldn't help it. Their love and support brought the tears again. I tried to laugh them away. "You guys love me, you have to say that."

Tessa frowned into the mirror at me. "No, Miranda. You *are* all those things. You have to find them in yourself, that's all."

"Let's just work on the doormat part," I said.

Sadie's eyes lit up, and she started jumping, even going so far as to raise her hand. "I know what she is! It just came to me! I know! I know!"

Kimy barked out, "Speak!"

Sadie took a deep breath, making sure all eyes were on her. "She's a…minx!"

"A what?" I asked. Wasn't that some sort of rodent animal like a squirrel? But I saw the dawning recognition in their eyes. They agreed with her.

Tessa stepped back. "Yes." She cocked her head to the side. "It's there, isn't it? Right under the surface."

I rolled my eyes, but Chloe chimed in, "Yeah. I mean, she's got it in spades. I never pushed the issue because, well, she was married to an ungrateful asshole. I didn't want her to feel worse when his narcissistic brain didn't notice."

Kimy grabbed my sleep shirt, pulling it tight around my middle. "She's still got a good rack and a smallish waist. And big butts are in style now." She patted my ass, and I slapped her hand away. Nodding in agreement with the others, she continued, "She could pull it off. And that air of klutzy innocence would really make the Doms drool."

She made squishy fingers toward my breasts, so I

slapped at her hands again. "Excuse me? What in the hell are you talking about?"

Laughing, Kimy met my gaze in the mirror. "How do you feel about getting spanked?"

I blushed crimson.

"I am not talking about that!" Tessa shooed Chloe away and led me to the chair. "I'm talking about a nice, decent man who will treat her with kindness and respect."

"Boring!" Chloe exclaimed, marching over to Tessa. "She's had vanilla. She needs variety. Maybe even a little chocolate. Or a strawberry."

"She's not into strawberry. Not even a little. She was mortified when she dropped the towel and I saw her naked. She's not bi," Kimy, who was bisexual, scoffed.

Bi? I thought they were talking ice cream–Oh! They began laughing at my expressive face. *Never could hide my emotions or lie, dammit.*

Sadie smiled softly. "Whoever we find for her must be careful not to damage her innocence. It's part of her charm."

They nodded in agreement, arguing amongst themselves as the realization hit me. I was their next "project". God help me, I didn't want a man, or a woman, or anything! I simply wished to be free and told them so. I was a doormat no more, therefore, I could speak up.

They guffawed, and Sadie explained, "Honey, we aren't getting you into a relationship. We're helping you find yourself."

"Through sex?" I squeaked.

"No!" Kimy growled. "Through interaction with people

on a social level. Not school fundraisers, PTA, or community volunteering."

"What's wrong with sex?" Chloe asked, fixing her lipstick in the mirror.

"I'm not going on Tenderizer or whatever. I can take care of my own business. And frankly, I'm looking forward to sleeping alone without anyone stealing the covers or snoring like a bear."

"They don't sleep over on Tinder," Kimy interjected. We turned as one to gawk at her. She shrugged.

Getting back to the matter at hand, I stated, "I need to focus on this separation and what I'm going to do about a living space. I have to be out by the time he gets back from the cruise."

The collective, "WHAT?!" had me cringing and holding my ears.

"It's in his name. Everything is. I haven't held a paying job since we got married. You know that."

For the first time ever, I saw Tessa lose her cool. Her eyes narrowed on me. "Did that rat bastard tell you that? That it was all his? That you get nothing? That you had to leave?"

I simply nodded.

An incensed Tessa was kind of *Stepford Wives* scary. "Well, we will certainly see about that. Illinois is a common law state. That means you get half, honey. Jerome will see to that and more." Jerome was Tessa's husband. One of Illinois' top attorneys. A ruthless bull in the courtroom and, according to Tessa, in the bedroom as well. They complemented each other perfectly, and she'd even let slip he was considering running for State Attorney General.

"I'm not sure Jerome would want to take on my divorce, honey."

"Don't be ridiculous. Of course, he will. He never really liked Rat Bastard anyway. He will get you half, plus alimony, and do it pro bono."

"Don't make promises, Tessa," Kimy warned.

"I'm not!" Tessa rounded on her. "I'm stating a fact. Jerome will take this on personally, or he *will* answer to me. It's a done deal. Besides, he loves Miranda almost as much as I do. Oh! He might have some suitable ideas for companions." Her eyes lit up, and she became sweet Tessa once more.

Kimy rolled her eyes. "I'll start doing some research on Illinois divorce cases, and maybe some research into Rat Bastard's private dealings in his job. Being a librarian at a college, you meet all sorts of folks, in addition, you have access to lots of information." She looked around. "He was either very frugal with his money or had a few not so legal dealings with his company."

"What?" I stood up. "He's never done anything shady that I know of."

"Exactly. That you know of. But you don't know a lot about his work, do you, honey?" Sadie sandwiched me between her hands and ran her Reiki moves up and down my body. "Your aura is much clearer, almost a lovely orange, but when he is near you, it's as if a grayness appears. His aura is very murky."

"Whatever," Kimy grumbled. "The point is, he's not getting off with everything. He's going to pay."

I stared at each one of them. Kimy scowled back.

Tessa's jaw was set in a stubborn line. Chloe nodded and winked at me. And Sadie, sweet Sadie, had her mantra book out and flipped to a page on making a voodoo doll for spiritual ease. I was in good hands. "OK, where do we start?"

Tessa linked her arm in mine. "With dinner, of course. I've prepared a lovely beef Wellington with parsley potatoes, a tasty Merlot, of course, and Napoleons that will melt in your mouth."

I followed them down the stairs and into my new life wondering if I should call a plumber about the bullet hole in my bathtub or leave it for Daniel…er, Rat Bastard. *Yeah, leave it for Rat Bastard!*

Chapter Two

"I'm sorry, Miranda, I don't know what to tell you. Illinois law states you and Rat Bastard have to be officially separated for six months before you can file for divorce, and divorce is through irreconcilable differences only." Tessa held my hands as she gave me the bad news. "There's more," she said. "You have to be legally separated and live in separate households."

"OK, well, what does that mean except that I have to exit the house as he said?"

"You don't have to. It would be probably best if you did. It will get even messier because your name isn't on the mortgage."

"He was right." I hung my head.

"Well, only for a little bit because the house will have to

be sold, and then, or if, you really want the house, you can buy it as part of the settlement deal."

"I don't know, it's all happening so fast. I'll have to think about it, but for now, I guess I need to find a place to stay. He's coming back tomorrow."

"I know it's not ideal, but you could stay in our guest-house. It's got everything including a kitchen, and it's on the other side of the pool so it's kind of like you're on your own."

Tessa, bless her, she was always thinking one step ahead of me. Grateful tears fell as I accepted. "But I will be out as soon as I figure out what I'm gonna do. I mean there's not a lot of calls for a fifty-something woman with no college education. You know the only skills I have are being a mom and a housewife. I mean I was a bookkeeper, but things have changed in the last couple of decades. I guess I could get a housekeeper job. Do you need a housekeeper?"

Tessa frowned at me. "You're doing it again. You have a lot of skills, a lot of experience in a lot of things. It's all in how you word it. You are definitely skilled in event planning, in product management, logistics, all sorts of things."

"Logistics?"

"Of course! You manage to get everybody to where they need to be on time all the time—that's logistics."

I laughed at her practicality and the way she twisted things. "Now, don't worry, I happen to be an expert resume writer, and we will get you a job you love in no time at all. In the meantime, the pool is right there, the guesthouse is fully stocked, including liquor, and you are taking a two-week vacation."

"I've taken two weeks."

"So, take two more. You deserve it after what Rat Bastard has put you through." Apparently, the grapevine had been humming with the news that Daniel and his new girlfriend were back and flaunting their relationship. I got sympathetic looks yesterday at the local market.

She got up and looked around the guest bedroom where I was temporarily ensconced, and when I noticed, I grumbled, "I couldn't stand to stay in the master bedroom after what Rat Bastard did. Who knows if he brought her to the house, to my bed while they were hiding their fling?"

"What is yours around here? I mean it's all been deco-rated by designer, right? It's got that, I don't know, plastic feel about it."

I didn't take offense; I understood what she meant. A designer had done everything because Daniel had insisted on the right touch for every room. I realized at that moment this really wasn't my home. "He purchased it. He got the new promotion. He felt he we needed a more modern look for VP of Finance. So, we moved from our cozy four-bedroom cottage next to the school, and our children had to grow up in this glass-enclosed mausoleum where everything was cool marble, leather, and chrome."

I scoffed, "Not even my clothes are my style. I had a personal shopper who he called whenever we were invited to a special event, and she brought me over what I was to wear. At the time, I thought it was simply more convenient because I didn't really care for shopping, but now I realize it was another piece of me he took away."

"So, you literally don't even have the clothes on your back."

I sighed. "Nothing except my photos and the mementos the children gave to me."

"Where are they?"

I pointed to the closet. "The pictures of the kids are up in the closet here in the guestroom, school pictures, picnics, family visits, those kinds of things. Those weren't allowed to mess up the ambiance, they were only mine, and of course, all of the little gifts the kids made me through the years."

I heard her mumble, "Rat Bastard" under her breath. She opened the guestroom closet and found it piled high with boxes which should have been on display in a real home.

Sauntering up behind her, I began pulling down boxes. "Did you ever wonder why we never hung out at my house? It was because he felt my friends weren't necessary, after all, I had him, and that should be enough. But I needed all of you. I fought for our monthly gatherings because I needed it to keep my sanity."

Tessa's eyes brimmed with tears. "You don't have to worry about ever losing us, Miranda. If you stop coming to us, we will go thru the gates of hell to bring you back where you belong." She hugged me. We had a short cry which only the best of friends can share, then we laughed at our runny mascara in the mirror.

"Well, since you are all packed up, it should be easy to load and haul over to our guesthouse," she said as she fixed her makeup. "I'll get some healthy college student to help out. You'll be out of here by tomorrow. Now, do you know if he's canceled your credit cards or any of your bank accounts?" I shook my head in the negative. "I have no idea. I've been holed up in here for the past week and a half."

"Well, let's see." She grabbed her purse, punched in a few numbers on her phone, and handed it to me. Apparently, Rat Bastard thought I really was a doormat. He hadn't bothered to take the money out of our joint account, so I did. I grabbed the cash from the savings account, too.

"Let's go shopping," I exclaimed with a smile. "Call the others. We can have a Miranda-Needs-A-New-Look Day."

With a gleeful giggle, very un-Tessa-like, we gathered the rest of the Goddesses and hit the shops. I was so thankful to have them with me since I was overwhelmed and didn't realize what I signed on for. When I said "makeover", boy did they make me over!

Gone was the extremely long brown hair. Now, I supported a bouncy shoulder-length bob in dark golden blonde with big copper streaks. The boring neutral color palette for my face was replaced with deep purple eye shadow to bring out the amber flecks in my green eyes, and bright red lipstick to show off my full, kissable lips. I was seaweed wrapped, Swedish massaged, and forced to drink some disgusting green concoction which promised to detox my insides and align my chakras. I prayed it wouldn't work immediately because I would never make it to the bathroom. Visions of a food poisoning scene from a girl movie flitted through my mind.

Then came the clothes—Victoria's Secret, Fredericks of Hollywood, Nordstrom's, Macy's, and so many small boutiques, I can't remember where I bought what. Except for a few items, Chloe had everything shipped to the guest-house at Tessa's. Even Kimy and Sadie had fun trying on some items. When we begin to slow down, we energized with Starbucks and a yummy lemon loaf.

"Well, Miranda, are you happy?" Sadie asked, sipping on her green tea chai.

"I'm getting there," I replied with a sigh. "It hurt the kids I think, but it was almost as if they could tell something wasn't right. They call me every day, and I think it helped them to know I am going to be living near Tessa since they are both out of state right now."

"Did you tell Jennifer about Megan?" Kimy asked.

"Yes, she has a right to know, and as Rat Bastard said, she's going to become the new Mrs. Blake. I wanted them to be prepared."

"I think you should change your name as well, Miran-da," Chloe stated.

"Yeah, Miranda's so not you," Sadie sighed. "You should be a Dawn or a Sunny, something bright like your aura."

Kimy rolled her eyes. "Not her first name, Sadie, her last. She doesn't need any ties to Rat Bastard."

I took a sip of my salted caramel cappuccino for strength. "I've been thinking about that, too. I'll switch it back to my maiden name after the divorce. But for now, Sadie's right. I need to change something. Miranda was my grandmother's name, but they called her Randi. She was amazing—she ran bootleg whiskey during Prohibition, married a younger man, and learned how to fly. She buried eight husbands. I'm afraid I've let her down with my life so far. If I'm going to start over, then a new me includes a new name. No more Miranda. I'm Randi!"

"Yes! Cheers to Randi!" Sadie grinned. "I'll check the name against my numbers chart, but I bet it will fit you perfectly!"

"To Randi!" The Goddesses clanked their glasses together.

"Well, I have some news to celebrate as well," Tessa stated with a twinkle in her eye. "You know that Jerome and I—"

Kimy interrupted her, "Do you always call him Jerome?" she asked. Flipping her short hair back, she gave a sultry look, imitating Tessa's accent. "Oh Jerome, darling, yes, that's it! Perfect! Ooh! Ooh! That's the ticket!!"

Chloe chimed in, "It's better than Jerry! That's the name of a car salesman with bad breath and a comb-over."

I bit my lip, trying not to laugh. Tessa was furious.

"Do you morons mind? I've got important news!" She flung her napkin down in irritation.

Giggles subsided as I shushed the others and told her, "Go on, sweetie. What's your news?"

"Thank you," she murmured with a nod at me, but her smile returned as she said, "We are approved for the adoption!"

Jumping from my chair, I squealed and ran to hug her. Sadie clapped, her bracelets clanging, and even Kimy grinned. Chloe raised her latte. "To Tessa and Jerome and their new bundle of joy!" I reached for my mug and toasted with the rest of them.

After our merriment subsided, Tessa said, "It's 'bundles'

actually. Oh, and really, it's a three-year-old boy and a one-year-old girl."

"Wow!" Two toddlers running around in her pristine home? That should be interesting.

Sadie, rather quiet for a change, took her hand. "You will be a wonderful mother, Tessa. I can see it."

We teared up. Tessa, who couldn't conceive, was now going to have not one, but two children. This called for more hugs and happy wishes.

"There is one thing," Tessa continued as she dried her eyes. "It's a bit complicated, but the boy is black, and the girl is white. The poor children were found in a condemned home in London with some others. It appeared to be a holding house of some sort."

"Trafficking?" Kimy growled.

Tessa nodded and reached for another tissue. "When they tried to separate the two of them, the boy attacked whoever came near. He was quite protective of the baby. I couldn't leave him, therefore, we adopted him, too."

We were silent for a moment, absorbing the enormity of evil in the world. Sadie grabbed our hands, spoke a quiet prayer for the children still waiting to be found.

Tessa broke the stillness, "Now, now, we've got plenty to be thankful for." She turned to Chloe. "And I expect a beautiful baby shower before we go over and get them."

"You got it, love! It's been a while since I threw a party." She glanced at me. "Speaking of partying…"

"Oh no!" I waved my hand in the negative. "I'm not ready for clubbing, or whatever you call it."

"But, Randi, you're looking pretty good–the hair, the

nails. I love that outfit. The simple red blouse with the black tight skirt, very rockabilly hipster," Chloe simpered. "Add those platform stilettos…" She winked at me.

"And that adorable hat I picked for you," Sadie chimed in.

"Don't forget the Audrey Hepburn sunglasses," Tessa declared, getting into the mood.

"And we have one hot minx strutting down the street," Kimy concluded, grinning like a Cheshire cat. "So, let's see it."

"See what?" I laughed.

"Get up! We wanna see you work it," Chloe sang, clapping her hands, "Work it, work it."

"You guys are crazy! We are sitting outside Starbucks at the Governors Mall and you want me to strut it like a hooker." I shook my head.

Sadie whooped. "Absolutely! Go, girl! Go, Randi! Get your groove on!" She pulled out my chair, and Chloe yanked me to my feet.

Tessa smiled and pointed down the block "Stroll that way, turn around, give us your best Miss America smile, and then come back." She shooed me with her hands.

Laughing, I walked the distance as well as I could in a tight skirt and five-inch stilettos. I didn't have to shake or wiggle it, my body sort of did it for me, *thank you*, but I did push my breasts out and tuck in my tummy for full effect.

I spun around, gave them a little peek above my glasses, then sashayed with exaggerated confidence back to my catcalling friends. I sauntered past them, tipping my hat and pushing out my ass. Unfortunately, tipping my hat down triggered momentary blindness in my right eye. Just then, the right heel of my new stilettos got caught in a hole in the sidewalk, causing me to pitch forward, falling with ill grace onto my knees and into the crotch of a total stranger. I heard the horrified gasp of the girls behind me.

Before I could even register an apology, he put his paper down on the table and stated, "Well, until now, I thought that falling at my feet thing was just something guys said."

I looked up into the most beautiful blue eyes I had ever seen. I was struck dumb by the gorgeous man staring down at me. Of course, after my mind returned, I went into full-blown Miranda the Klutz mode, stammering an apology as I scrambled—with difficulty—to get off the sidewalk and back on my broken heels. Unfortunately, I needed leverage, so I leaned a little too hard on the hand which was too close to the man's jean-clad scrotum. With a yelp of pain, he flung off my hand, I lost my balance and fell once again on my ass.

This time, however, my friends were there to help me up. I stumbled out of my shoes and walked barefoot, fully humiliated, back to the car with Sadie, Kimy, and Chloe murmuring words of comfort. Tessa had stayed behind to clean up the social mess, I guess.

"Randi" was off to a clumsy start.

Chapter Three

"It wasn't as bad as you think," Tessa assured me as she helped me unpack the new things we purchased on our girls' day. We were in the bedroom of my new "home", aka her guesthouse.

"Honey, I tried to be sexy. I fell on my ass after I landed face-first in the crotch of the most handsome man ever, and I decided to ruin it by using his balls as leverage to get up!" I wailed.

Tessa laughed. "Honestly, Ritter found you charming. He's a complete rogue, and normally, I say steer clear, but I think you need a guide to boost your confidence. He wanted your number, ergo, I gave it to him."

"You what?" I screeched turning away from the closet. "How could you do that? He's probably ten years younger than me! I'm not ready. I've got to figure out me before I figure out me and a man…if I even want another one."

"And that's exactly why you need Ritter—no relationship just fun and sex. Good sex for once, not that stuff Rat Bastard put you through."

"He barely touched me, Tessa, after the kids were born."

"Exactly! You need a man to get you all fired up and melt your butter", she exclaimed, turning pink.

"Why, Tessa, I think you're blushing," I drawled at her honesty. "Though I wouldn't know what to do with a man like that. He's obviously well out of my league."

"He's fine; he's carefree. And what's so bad about going out on one date? You don't have to sleep with him," she argued, stepping up to me. She was getting riled up, and I had to suppress my grin because she reminded me of a pesky butterfly, fluttering her bejeweled fingers.

"So, he's going to call you, and you're going to call us, and we are going to make you up and get you some confidence, and maybe a little drunk. Then you're going to meet this guy, and you're gonna laugh over your little faux pas, and you're going to have a wonderful time. OK?"

"OK. You have a deal, but I bet he doesn't call."

I WAS WRONG. He called that afternoon. "Hello! Is this the ball-busting beautiful blonde I met earlier at the café?"

I almost dropped the phone. That sexy voice made me

quiver. "Oh, yes! This is me...er...I mean, this is Mira... er...Randi."

"Well, hello, Randi. This is Ritter Michaels. I was wondering if you would like to have dinner with me tonight."

I hesitated. Was I even ready for this? No, but I still wanted to go.

"Come on, Randi," he cajoled. "I don't like to eat alone, and you owe me. I finally have a beautiful woman falling into my lap, and she crushes my spirit–for lack of a better word–by running away."

I took a deep breath and embraced my inner Randi. "Very well. Where would you like to meet?"

He mentioned a restaurant close to the Michigan Avenue nightlife. "I'll set the reservations for seven," he said.

"I'll see you then," I stammered before I lost my nerve.

"Oh, and, Randi?" He spoke seductively, "Feel free to wear that hat."

I hung up on his chuckle and sank onto the bed, glancing at the clock on the wall. I was going on my first date since my divorce, and I had less than four hours. *Oh shit!* Time to get ready.

Chloe and Kimy came to my aid. Tessa was helping Jerome host a fundraising dinner for his campaign, and Sadie was apparently exorcizing a ghost from a large house in Hoffman Estates.

After a bit of discussion on what constituted the proper attire, I decided on the traditional little black dress, however, I pumped it up with my fancy new shoes, a statement necklace, and, of course, the hat. Here was hoping I wouldn't trip this time, although, he didn't seem to mind.

I arrived at the restaurant, nerves and all, at 7:05. The maître di smiled, leading me through the tables into a private area. As soon as I came into view, Ritter stood, all sophisticated and charming. *Yep, I could get used to this.*

"You look gorgeous," I blurted, flushing furiously as he chuckled and the maître di silently disappeared.

"I believe that was my line, but thank you," he replied, ushering me into the quiet booth.

"I'm sorry. I'm a bit nervous," I mumbled.

He reached for my hand, and I felt the warmth of his fingers close around mine. "Don't be. I find you charming and refreshing. I'd like to get to know you better."

I blushed, all sorts of quivering things happening down below.

"How about a drink?" he suggested.

"What are you having?"

"I'm having Scotch on the rocks." I shook my head in the negative. "Do you like wine?"

"Yes."

He turned to the waiter. "Bring us an Il Paradiso di Manfredi Rosso di Montalcino 2014."

"Very good, Sir." He slipped away.

Ritter took a sip of his drink. "Tessa tells me you're newly divorced and looking to live life to the fullest. How can I help?" He was still holding my hand, rubbing his thumb on the inside of my wrist. Between the sexy voice and the physical contact, I almost climbed across the table and onto his lap.

He grinned slightly as if he could read my thoughts. I took a moment to get a grip and tried to pull my hand away, but he grasped it firmly. "Don't be shy; tell me what I can do."

I searched for something which didn't involve both of us naked in a bed. "A job," I blurted out and then attempted more calmly, "I need a job." I sat back, completely mortified once again.

"You are priceless, Randi," he chuckled. "I might actually have something for you." The way he said it– smooth and dark, eyeing at me intently–well, to be honest, it sort of gave me an uneasy feeling.

"I am looking for actual work," I attempted to clarify.

He laughed out loud, and I took the moment to retract my hand. "Oh, Randi, love, you are a treasure." He took a long swallow, finishing his drink, signaling the waiter for another. "I meant that I can see if there is something in my company. My brother Reed and I own Michaels Group."

I made the connection at once. This wasn't just any Ritter Michaels, this was the entire conglomerate Michaels family. Buying and selling real estate, importing and exporting goods and services, and they had their fingers in the pies of everything, including the newest technology. I was so out of my league here.

I almost knocked over the water glass, bringing it to my lips and taking a big drink to clear my throat. "OK then, I should send you my resume," I croaked, ingesting another gulp of water.

The sommelier brought back the wine, and after tasting it and approving, Ritter poured me a hefty glass. "You do that, Randi. On another topic, I hope you don't mind, but I've taken the liberty of ordering something special for the evening. The chef prepared it especially for us."

Praying it wasn't some sort of octopus, eel, or something, I nodded. "That sounds lovely."

He chuckled. "Your expression says otherwise."

I couldn't help the blush; therefore, I took a sip of wine instead. We talked books and movies, and if he name-dropped a bit too much, well, he was entitled. We were beginning to discuss the latest local politics when our meal arrived, and my smile widened. "How did you know?" I asked.

"Tessa told me if I wanted to impress you, to order this. She's a fountain of information. It's your favorite, right?"

I stared down at the absolutely mouth-watering bacon cheeseburger and hot fries before me.

"Dig in," he encouraged.

"Is this going to upset the chef?" I asked as I picked up a fry.

"If it is, he'll get over it. I own the restaurant. I tell him to make something, he makes it."

I snickered and took a hefty bite of my burger. It was absolute heaven. Amid the bites, we continued our discussion of local politics, the economy, and events. We had quite a few things in common, and I began to relax.

A shadow fell across the table, and I peered up into the dark eyes of another handsome man accompanied by an equally stunning woman at his side. "Hello, Ritter. How nice to see you. I didn't know you were going to be here tonight."

Ritter stood up, shaking the man's hand. He glanced at

me as he introduced me to the stranger, "This is Randi Blake. Randi, this is my brother, Reed Michaels."

Reed extended his hand, and I took it, feeling the firm handshake, and my pulse quickened. I quickly let go, but he continued to stare at me. "Sorry, have we met before?"

"You do seem vaguely familiar," the woman said. She extended her hand as well. "Hello, my name is Lauren, Lauren Livingston."

Oh, the famous designer! Her fingers barely touched mine. I suddenly felt like the wallflower I was.

"I believe I've seen you with the wife of Jerome."

"Yes, Tessa is a dear friend," I stated.

"How nice for you." She flicked off a small piece of nonexistent lint on Reed's suit lapel. "We really must be going, Reed."

Reed acknowledged her with a nod. "It was lovely to meet you, Randi. Ritter, I'll see you at the office tomorrow. Have a lovely evening."

Miranda watched the beautiful couple walk away. *Bet she's never fallen in her heels.*

"And that, my dear, was my older brother. He runs the corporation. I'm simply a mere errand boy." He laid a hand over his heart.

I laughed at his self-deprecating humor. "I don't see you as an errand boy. They make a lovely couple."

"Yes, they've been friends forever. She's dying to get her claws into him and all of his money," Reed whispered theatrically. "She might actually manage it. He's not getting any younger."

Since he appeared to be around my age, I quickly

changed the subject. "What are your hobbies?" He looked at me for a moment, annoyance flickering in his eyes. Finally, he laughed and said, "My hobbies are the same as every playboy: wine, women, and fast cars."

"I think there's a bit more to you."

"I do enjoy digging at my brother, too."

"I thought as much, sibling rivalry and all that."

"Precisely, my dear Randi."

This last was said with a bit of a slur. Ritter enjoyed his whiskey, but I hoped he wasn't driving.

Dinner finished, the waiter appeared with a platter. "Ah, coffee and an absolutely luscious cheesecake that the chef has prepared. Bring it on, my good man!" Ritter spoke loudly.

I offered a small grin, personally relieved the coffee had arrived. Ritter needed to sober up in my opinion.

"This has been absolutely fantastic. I can't remember a dinner where I laughed so much. Thank you, dear Randi." He raised his once again empty glass in a toast.

I couldn't help the blush. "You're quite welcome, Ritter, and thank you for being such a gentleman and forgiving my faux pas.

After eating dessert and drinking a whole pot of coffee between the two of us, it was time to leave. I still wasn't sure Ritter was sober enough and prayed he wouldn't be the one driving tonight.

As we waited for the valet outside, our waiter approached. "Madam, the chef has prepared a doggy bag for you."

I peeked inside, finding the lovely cheesecake resting in a

nice foil pan. "Tell him thank you. Dinner was delicious." The waiter smiled and returned inside.

"It appears you charmed everyone here. Perhaps you do need to come to work for us. It's a dull and boring place."

I snickered. "I'll send you the resume, but be warned, I've been a mother and housewife for twenty-five years. I'm a bit out of the loop."

He held up his hand. "You have taken a directorial position for the past twenty-five years." He ticked off a finger. "You are experienced in nursing, home healthcare, financing, catering." He started on the other hand. "Event planning, operational expertise, and human resources."

"Sure, that's what it is." My car appeared, and I reached my hand out to shake his, but he pulled me in for a tight hug and kissed me lightly on the cheek. The scent of his aftershave did a funny thing to my brain, giving me the wildest urge to grab his face and press his lips to mine, but as he moved closer, an image of Reed entered my mind. I stepped back, and the moment ended.

"You'll hear from me, Randi. Have a good night."

I moved to my car on wobbly legs and drove off into the night realizing I would have sweet dreams this evening. But would they be about Ritter or his older brother, Reed?

Chapter Four

"Well, how did it go?"

I answered the phone at six o'clock in the morning to find the ever-perky Chloe demanding to know about my date. "Went fine. Call me later," I mumbled into the receiver."

"Oh my God! Is he there?" She let out an excited squeal that pierced my ears.

"No!" I said and hung up, making a mental note to talk to her about her teenage squeaks.

Three hours later, refreshed from a shower, a cup of coffee, and some hideous egg frittata thing that was supposed to be good for me, I answered the door to my four best friends.

They clambered in with shouts and yells, hugs and

kisses, and a variety of bangles, bells, and incense. However, they brought me Starbucks, so I smiled as they ran into the kitchen talking a mile a minute. I tried to understand the words they were saying, and my heart swelled. It was good to have friends.

"OK, Miss Grumpypants, now tell us," Chloe demanded as she handed me an apple fritter and that luscious mug of caramel macchiato.

"This is in celebration," Tessa pointed to the delicious fried concoction, "and tomorrow it's back on the diets, ladies."

"Yes, Ma'am," Kimy bit into a muffin the size of her grande cup. "Now details!"

"It went fine. He was a gentleman. We had a good time. He kissed me on the cheek."

Kimy grimaced. "No little squeeze, a tush grab, nothing?"

"Oh my God, what century do you live in?" Have you not heard of the 'me too' movement?" Chloe scowled.

"Men don't do that anymore. Thank God. It's disgusting." Tessa shuddered.

"I don't know. Personally, I don't mind a little tushy grab every once in a while," Sadie said. "It's sort of like a little unexpected compliment."

Chloe rolled her eyes. "Whatever. Is he going to call? Is he going to see you again? Did you set up another date?"

"No, we didn't set up another date. I thanked him for a lovely evening, he kissed my cheek, made sure I got in my car with no issues, and he left." I whipped around to Kimy.

"Make sure you have a serious talk with Sadie about predators, would you?"

Sadie huffed, but Kimy nodded and continued the interrogation, "How late was it?"

"Ten."

"You got in at ten?" Kimy pushed back her plate. "Well, that's depressing."

I waved a hand in front of her face. "Hi, remember me? I'm not into one-night stands. I don't even know if I could do a one-night stand."

Tessa nodded in agreement. "Absolutely! A lady never does it on the first date."

I noted the storm clouds gathering in Chloe and Kimy's eyes, and I intervened from an imminent argument over social semantics in the modern world. "I had a lovely time. It was exactly what I needed to dip my toe in the pool, so to speak, and I think it went quite well."

"OK, what's next?"

"I need to go to the grocery store."

"No, I mean with your life? What are you going to do?" Tessa inquired.

"I don't know. I've got to find a job, I know that."

"Well then, let's work on pumping up your resume," Chloe slapped her hands on the granite countertop. "Where's your tablet?"

I smiled softly thinking of what Ritter said about my domestication skills. "What's that look for? What are you not telling us?" Sadie was peering intently into my face, and I shooed her away.

"It's nothing. Just a little conversation that Ritter and I had at dinner about how to make the best of the qualities and the skills I do possess. He even said he might be able to help me find one."

"That's a perfect opening for him to call you again!" Chloe clapped her hands in such glee, I thought she might execute a back tuck onto the coffee table. You could take the cheerleader out of high school, but…

"That is not what that means," I argued.

"It is, too," she insisted, gazing Kimy for confirmation, who simply shrugged.

"It could be," Kimy conceded.

I began to blush at the thought. "I'm not holding my breath, now pass me another apple fritter."

THREE DAYS LATER, I heard from Ritter.

"Hello," I panted, trying to work through the newest set of the *Yoga Booty Ballet* DVDs Chloe had given me. I refused to take the ones on pole dancing she wanted me to try.

"Why, Randi dear, you sound positively breathless. Have I called at an inopportune moment?" he chuckled.

The sexual innuendo did not slip past me, neither did the immediate pool of warmth to my nether regions. "No, simply keeping in shape." I reached for my water.

"And what a delightful shape it is, Randi."

Oh boy! Charmingly cheesy. "What can I do for you, Ritter?" I wiped the sweat from my upper lip.

"Well that just opens up a wealth of possibilities," he

said smoothly. "However, this call is about what *I* can do for *you*. My colleague at the conglomerate, Matthew Hartley, has an opening for an executive assistant. I immediately thought of you. You didn't send me your resume, but I've talked you up, and he wants an interview."

"Thank you, Ritter, but I don't think I'm executive assistant material. I'm just now getting back into the workforce."

"Don't be ridiculous, you're perfect for the job. You know how to run things, you know how to keep to a schedule, you're fine. Matt is totally unorganized. His assistant basically keeps him in line, so he doesn't get fired. The other departments handle the harder stuff."

"What about specific software programs you might use?"

"We'll train you. Don't worry, I'll be with you every step of the way."

Thinking about his boast, I had a feeling what Ritter actually knew about software programs could probably be fit in a teacup. I nevertheless agreed to meet with his colleague at three o'clock tomorrow afternoon at the Michaels Group headquarters.

That night, I called an emergency meeting of the ladies, a quick what-to-wear gathering complete with a meeting about the resume, along with a much-needed confidence boosting session. Oh, and I mustn't forget the tea leaves, psychic reading, horoscope, numbers, and runes strewn across the kitchen table. I felt adequately prepared for my very first job interview in over twenty-five years.

THE NEXT AFTERNOON, I stepped into the massive lobby of the Michaels Group, walked up to the front desk, and asked for Mr. Matthew Hartley. I had an appointment and was quickly directed into the elevator and up to the 21st floor. I checked my appearance in the confines on the mirrored wall. Navy blue suit, pin-striped blouse, and nude heels made me look confident, even if I didn't feel it.

As I exited the elevator, I a lovely young woman met me there to inform me Mr. Hartley was in a meeting and would be with me shortly. She also asked if I would like water or coffee or tea while I waited. I declined, although, I really could use a glass of water. *What if I started coughing in there? I should have taken the water.* I started to call out to her…but then thought that if I drank the water, I might have to pee during the interview. *That could be terribly uncomfortable.* Maybe a little coffee to calm my nerves? *Caffeine heightens your nerves. Definitely no coffee.* And tea, for some unfathomable reason, did weird things to my stomach. *Yeah, that would be the way to make a first impression. Smelly gas and sewer burps.*

After what seemed like a lifetime, the receptionist ushered me in to see Mr. Matthew Hartley. He barely looked old enough to be behind his desk much less running a department. Feeling older than dirt, I extended my hand and stumbled slightly in my too high heels. He reached out to grab me, his hand landing on my boob, and he dropped me like a hot potato. My hip hit the arm of the sofa as I fell, and that was my salvation. I bounced against the leather, righted myself, and managed to only slightly twist my ankle. Mr. Hartley was safely ensconced behind his large desk as if he hadn't only moments ago inadvertently copped a feel; therefore, I took my cue from him, and quietly sat down in the nearest chair.

"Well, Ms. Blake, Ritter has told me some lovely things about you. I'm glad you could take the interview. Tell me what qualifications do you possess to work with the Michaels Group?"

I rattled off what I could do professionally, polishing up the meager skills I had, remembering exactly what Chloe and Kimi told me to say in a professional capacity along with social skills I had memorized. I thought I was doing pretty well and totally ignored Sadie's thoughtful offer to pass along a free psychic reading if I got the job.

"It certainly seems you are qualified. You're hired."

"Excuse me, shouldn't I take a test or something?"

"If Ritter says you're a go, you're a go. You saw my secretary. She's about to pop with that baby."

What an odd thing to say. Rather unprofessional. Even given his age.

"Yeah, well, I need somebody to take her place until she gets back. When she's back, I'm sure there's more than enough work for the two of you. She's gonna desire time off with the kid later too, so it'll be best to have somebody that can fill in all the time."

"I understand." I did, but I felt his casual manner was unprofessional, to say the least.

"I'm sure this will work out perfectly." He stood up,

signaling the end of the interview. I got to my feet as well, and we shook hands. After that, he pulled me in for a hug. *Extremely odd.* "Nice to have you on board. I'll get Suzanne. She can take it from there and get all setup and the ball rolling. When can you start?" He opened the door without waiting for an answer. "Suzanne!"

I jumped as he yelled into the outer office, but collected myself quickly. *It was going to be interesting, working for him.* "I can start immediately."

"Good, then we will see you tomorrow for training because you never know when Suzanne's gonna pop that kid out."

"Yes. Thank you very much for the opportunity."

"Think nothing of it. Here's Suzanne. Suzanne, this is Randi; she's going to be taking your place until you get back. Randi, this is Susanne." Mr. Hartley pivoted back into his office and firmly closed the door behind him.

I extended my hand. "Hello, I'm Miranda."

Suzanne ignored my hand, looked me up and down, and exclaimed, "You're not what I was expecting."

People were certainly refreshingly honest here. "I'm not?"

She shrugged. "I was expecting a blonde bimbo or one of Ritter's gals, but you might actually know what I'm talking about in this department. Matt has a way of speaking which sometimes rubs people the wrong way, but he has a good heart. Actually, I can't even say that. He only tries to cop a feel a few times a week. We're stuck with him, well, at least you are. I'm gone in a few weeks, and I may not come back."

Wow, OK, this is definitely different, but I've been out of the work-

force for twenty-five years, maybe it was normal to be so casual with your words. And what about that whole sexual harassment vibe? In any event, I called the girls to tell them the news while I breathed a sigh of relief. I was a working woman now!

The next day, I was at the office fifteen minutes early and handing a steaming cup of coffee and a donut to the large man at the security desk. "My first day here," I explained. "Wish me luck!"

He nodded and smiled. "You don't need luck, you got donuts." He waved me to the elevators.

Maybe some things were still the same after twenty-five years. I headed up to the 21st floor and my new boss. I saw Suzanne first.

"Let me get your W-4 employment form. I'm supposed to inform you they do a background check, drug test, and all that kind of stuff," She babbled, leading me down the hall to the supply room.

We spent the rest of the day going from department to department. The company had its own doctor, nurse… everything including a daycare. "That's gonna be great for you," I commented.

"You think I'm leaving my kid here? Oh no no no no no. I actually want my child. Between you and me, I mean you're older, you're not gonna have any kids or whatever. I don't care for the lady who runs it. No one does, but it's free. it comes with the benefits, so we put up with it. I heard she doesn't even like children. I don't know why she's involved in it other than she was one of Ritter's castoffs, and Reed had to find something for her to do, or she was gonna go public with how his brother treated her."

Oh goodness, I was getting quite a bit of information.

"Matthew and Ritter are polo buddies, golf buddies, and just buddy buddies. More than likely when you see one, you'll see the other. OK? And one of my tasks is usually to alert them when Reed heads this way. You understand what I'm saying?"

"Sure." I really didn't like the sound of this.

She glanced my way with a funny expression. "How long have you been out of the workforce?"

"Twenty-five years."

She rolled her eyes. "Great. I'm due in two days, and they give me somebody who can't even work the programs. Bet the last time you were in an office they had DOS."

"I know more than that," I retorted sharply.

"Well, thank God because when he said he was hiring an old lady, I didn't know what I was going to do. I mean not that you're old, it's just—"

I cut her off and said, "I understand. I'm definitely older than you, but I believe I can handle it."

"Then let me give you a tour of the place."

She introduced me to the various department heads and staff I might need for specific projects, showed me where all of the departments were, and the various sectors located in the home office.

We arrived back at her desk around two. "OK, so that's probably it for today. I really wanna go home anyway. My feet are killing me from hauling this kid around. The only place you haven't visited is Reed's office, and his office is obviously at the top. You really won't have a whole lot to do with him. He does come down occasionally to talk to Ritter or Matthew, but usually, he's holed up in his own private sanctum."

I nodded, feeling a bit disappointed I wouldn't run into him today.

"If you do see him just remember to be polite and get him whatever he requests. He probably won't even notice you, but Matthew and Ritter both require that heads up when he's heading their way. Basically, if you hear the ping of his private elevator—it has a different sound from ours— you get on the line no matter what, and you get Ritter and Matthew back here pronto if they are still in the building. Reed Michaels doesn't like to be kept waiting.

"Understood." I smiled at the young woman. "Now, let's get you off your feet and back at home where you can relax. I think I've got this for the rest of the day.

"I'm sure you do." She grinned back. "After all, you're used to running around after kids, and that's all they are."

I HAD JUST GOTTEN HOME, kicked off those horrible high heeled shoes, and poured myself a nice chardonnay when Tessa popped in. "Hi, love. I won't keep you. I bet you had quite a day. How did it go?" She puttered around the kitchen, heating up something that smelled divine. God love her, she brought me dinner.

"It went fine."

"I think it went more than fine." From behind her back, she produced a vase filled with flowers. "These arrived for you before you even got home."

I knew you'd get the job–Ritter was scrawled across the card.

"That's sweet," I said.

"I definitely know you're going to enjoy this job," Tessa gushed as she poured herself a glass of my wine. "I've heard it's a challenge for just one person."

"Oh, don't I know it. Suzanne was run ragged with those two, well technically, she works for Matthew, but half the time Ritter comes down needing something he doesn't want Reed to find out about, so he bypasses his secretary, who Reed hired, and goes to Suzanne."

"You better rethink that philosophy, honey. Reed is the head, not Ritter."

I nodded in agreement. Better to let Suzanne field that quagmire.

"Relax and have some dinner." She pushed a plate of pork tenderloin, mashed garlic potatoes, and broccoli toward me. "I'll get you set up for the rest of the week."

"OK," I mumbled through a to-die-for spoonful of mashed potatoes, "but no more heels. I about died today. I seriously thought I was going to wear my feet down to the nubs.

"Baby steps," she laughed. "You just have to get used to them.

"I have little feet and big boobs, balancing on the balls of my feet for eight hours a day, walking around, it doesn't work, Tessa."

"Honey, I haven't felt my feet in years. You just do what you got to do."

After Tessa left, I had a nice hot bath, soaked my sore

toes in some Epsom salts, and begged them to forgive me for what I did to them today before crawling into bed.

I was surprised I slept soundly, but a good job, the possibility of another date...you would have thought little 'old doormat Miranda' was actually living her life.

Chapter Five

I fell into the routine rather quickly. There really wasn't much to do; Suzanne was quite right. I practically babysat Matt, but I did get to see Ritter several times a day. While charming, I realized it would never be more than friendship. The snap flash of chemistry I first experienced with him disappeared.

The more I got to know Ritter, the more I thought he would be a lot of fun on occasion, but I didn't believe I could really keep up with his level of entertainment.

Reed, on the other hand, was another matter. Always professional, always polite, and always in a hurry. Most of the time, I didn't even have a chance to open the door or announce him. I suppose I would get better at it, but until that day came, Matt and Ritter were going to have to make sure their conversations weren't about Reed.

Suzanne was blessed with a bouncing baby boy on her due date. After a few days, she declared motherhood was wonderful and staying home all the time was not bad, however, when she hit the eight-week mark, she wanted to come back to work. With her impending return, I wasn't really sure what I would be doing or if I was going to keep my job.

At work, I kept to myself and did what was required of me. That said, my curious mind did wonder why Ritter, on occasion, hurried into Matt's office without acknowledging me, closing the door firmly behind him.

It was on one such instance I saw Reed coming around the corner. Remembering for once that I needed to alert them and knowing that he wouldn't answer the phone if I buzzed, I hurried to the door. Not thinking, I opened it suddenly without knocking. What I heard had me standing frozen in shock.

"How much longer do I need to keep this up, Ritter. I mean she's fine, but she's old and kind of klutzy. At least Suzanne, even pregnant, didn't trip over everything in sight." *It was only once, and I did because you left your damn gym bag in the middle of your office floor.* "I mean, she can't even manage to keep me posted before Reed barges in."

"It's just a little longer. OK? She's doing a good job, and you know how Reed sneaks up on people. She's new, she'll get used to it. Besides, we have to focus on the end game."

"No one ever learns anything nice by eavesdropping," Reed whispered behind me.

I shrieked, stumbling on my heels. He caught my elbow, preventing me from falling, and helped to straighten me up before marching into Matt's office with me in tow. "She tried to warn you, but you were too busy talking about her to notice her standing in the doorway." Reed let me go. "They know I'm here, Miranda, so you can leave."

I scooted out the door as fast as my heels would let me. Reed closed the door, and I breathed a sigh of relief, flopping down in my desk chair. It was then I noticed the door had not been completely closed. Getting up, I planned to rectify the mistake but thought better of it. *Maybe I could find out what was really going on between these brothers.* I opened the door a smidge more.

"Reed, sorry. We were…" *I couldn't make out what Matt was blubbering on about.*

"I know, don't worry about it. I've got bigger things to talk about as I'm sure you do, too. There's no sense gossiping about your secretary with her barely an arm's length away. As far as a little slap and tickle, nowadays, gentleman, that will get us in hot water quickly, so let's keep that to the bars or where no one can eavesdrop."

I blushed because of my current position right outside the door, and I had a feeling was fully aware of it.

"So, what can we do for you, Reed?" Ritter stepped up to his brother, and I realized the comparisons between the two could easily be seen from this angle. Ritter had that boyish charm down, and yet, he bristled with insolence whenever Reed stood in the same room. Reed, on the other hand, seemed to purposely stand in a less confrontational pose as he gazed at his younger brother.

"I need a favor. I need to borrow Miranda for the foreseeable future. I hear Suzanne is wanting to come back to work."

"You weren't sure what you were going to do with Miranda from what I understand." He looked pointedly at Matt. "She seems to do her job efficiently, although, she's not very good at keeping tabs on me. This should make it a little easier. She'll be working with my executive secretary on the fundraising campaign we have planned in celebration of our hundred-year anniversary. You won't mind, will you, Matt?"

"No, no, of course not," Matt hastened to reply. "It will be good to have Suzanne back."

Reed stared at him for a minute. "Yes, I'm sure it will be." He shifted his attention to Ritter. "Any objections, Ritter?"

"Miranda is a lovely person. I'm sure she can help in any way you may need."

Reed nodded and spun around to walk out. I hastened back over to my desk, sitting down as the door opened. Reed spoke, "By the way, Matt, if you ever speak to another employee in those terms again, I'll fire you. I don't need a harassment lawsuit. The company is one-hundred-years-old. You're not invaluable. Good day, gentlemen." He marched past me, leaving the door open and heading for the elevators.

I peeked into the office and found both men whispering furiously. Closing the door with a decisive click, I returned to my job, wondering what this next chapter would offer me.

I called the girls over that night for impromptu mani-pedis and we sat discussing the latest development.

"I think he likes you," Chloe said.

"I hate to disappoint you but he barely acknowledges me. He's simply decided that Agnes is an older woman, and she could use some help, because even though she's organized, there is a lot to do," I corrected. However, Agnes was known to be a taskmaster.

Sadie chimed in, "I think you're prettier and also your boss was bashing you, therefore, Reed made this up, and now, you're going to have to face that dragon of an executive assistant he has."

"Well, I think, as I know Reed, it is probably a bit of all of those things," Tessa replied. "He does need the help. He believes she can handle the dragon. He believes she must be organized in order to take care of Matt and his craziness, and there's something very compassionate about Reed."

Kimy snorted. "He's a cold fish. He lives for money, lives for the business, and he even dates cold fish like Lauren Livingston."

"Even cold fish have to populate," Chloe pointed out.

I ignored Chloe. "When Ritter and I went to dinner—that's when I first met Reed—he was with a woman named Lauren."

"Yeah, she's his type all right, just as cold and ruthless as he is. If they are together, it's because they are planning something, and I don't mean a sweet marriage. I mean a marriage of convenience. American money, a marriage of power...if that's what they're contemplating," Chloe stated.

Sadie shuddered. "Without love?"

"In the past, that's how it was done. Little thought was paid to emotion," Tessa explained.

I felt slightly sick. Reed wasn't cold. He was reserved and deserved someone who understood him. "He's been very kind to me, especially today."

"I know that look, Miranda. You are not thinking of having sweet thoughts on Reed are you?" Chloe narrowed her eyes at me.

I blushed. I couldn't help it.

"Trading one brother for the other? How very naughty!" Kimy crowed.

"Are we brother hopping Miranda?" Chloe said with a sly smile.

"Sounds kinky!" Sadie waggled her eyebrows.

"No," I denied.

"Although I like him very well as a person, Reed is not the marrying kind, and whether you think you're a minx or not, you are not ready to be romantic with your boss," Tessa stated. "You're more like me. You find a man, you stick with it. You don't go hopping from bed to bed or brother to brother."

"Or maybe you do, and you find out they like to share, and you're in brother sandwich heaven!" Chloe exclaimed.

"No, don't do it, Miranda," Sadie whispered in my ear. "The cards have one man picked for you."

I rolled my eyes at the idea that Sadie thought I was going to try and seduce both brothers. "All right, there's no need to worry. I'm telling you Reed simply needed my help."

I repeated that statement to a rather harried and to be truthful, offended Agnes Whipple, Reed's executive assistant. "Reed tells me that you are to assist me." She looked me up and down as if taking my measure.

"Yes, I'm to help you in whatever is needed in the planning of the hundred-year anniversary bash for the company." She appeared to be about 20 years older than me, but truth be told, she scared the living daylights out of me.

She met my eyes. "You one of Ritter's cast-offs?"

That was highly insulting, and my voice showed it when I spoke, "I was the interim secretary for Mr. Hartley. As I'm sure you're aware, his secretary, Suzanne, gave birth and should be returning to work within the week."

"Yes, Suzanne will be back in soon making sure that Matt knows all about Reed when he pops in. That's one thing in your favor. You never told that pompous ass when Reed was coming. Now, whether that was because you weren't observant enough or because you didn't feel that was your duty, I suppose it's not my business."

I didn't know how to respond; instead, I simply nodded. The next few hours were nervous, torturous and at some points, terrifying. Agnes may be nearing seventy-years-old, but she had the mind of a shark, the acerbic wit of a satirist, and no-nonsense barking voice of a drill sergeant. I was glad when Friday, came although, I must say, I was beginning to notice her peculiarities and got one step ahead of her on most of the projects, which was no easy feat. She really was unbelievably agile, but then again, she'd been with Reed for a long time.

By the end of the month, things were moving somewhat smoothly, to the point, Agnes said one day that she would hand the project over to me. I was nonplussed. "Thank you very much. I'm glad my performance has made you proud."

"I didn't say that, but I have too much work to do, and

since you haven't screwed up anything drastically to the point it can't be fixed…yet, I'm going to assume you actually want this job. God knows why, but you're good at it." The twinkle in her eyes belied the stern words. That was Agnes.

"I try." Hands on hips, I gave her a sassy grin.

She snorted and waved me away. "Get back to work."

And so I began checking out catering companies, double checking the menu, making sure the announcement had the perfect phrasing, getting the deal of the decade on linens, selected silverware, fine china, and crystal. I designed the ice sculpture, learned the ins and outs of sophisticated business party favors, and even took a class on how to fold napkins into different shapes. I loved every bit of it.

It brought me here in fact. I was once again at the Governor's Mall during my lunch hour. This time grabbing my present for Tessa's baby shower happening on Saturday. A local craft shop did custom music boxes, and I had them made a beautiful music box piano with a tiny teddy bear playing Ebony and Ivory. Yes, those were the names Tessa had been informed the children had been given. I also included a giant panda stuffed animal to be delivered–no way I was carrying that thing around.

In addition to picking up the gifts though, I had another errand to run for the anniversary party. I ducked into Leatherbound Paper Company to check on the invitations for the anniversary party. As I walked out, I happened to notice Reed and Lauren in a heated debate near the coffee shop. I'm not sure what made me do it, but I hid behind a huge potted plant to watch the show.

"Lauren, I thought I'd made it abundantly clear on

numerous occasions, the manipulation does not work with me. You can have your tantrums, you can stomp your foot, you can threaten whatever you think you have on me in order to sway me, but we are not going into business together. I will not buy your company, will not get you out of that mess, and will not mix business with pleasure."

"You are constantly mixing business with pleasure. I can't count the women you've employed because of Ritter's wandering dick. You've even got his latest throwaway, that fat cow, working with Agnes!" she screeched.

"Who I employ and my reasons for doing so are none of your business, Lauren, and if you speak about Miranda in those terms again, we are finished."

"Maybe we're finished now, Reed! I'm tired of not being a priority in your life! I need love and compassion!"

"No, you wish I would cater to your whims," he stated with no emotion. "Now, if you wish, you can end our affair, but I would love to have you as my hostess for the hundred-year anniversary. If not, I'm sure I can find someone else to take your place."

I shuddered. He sounded so cold, and I almost felt sorry for Lauren. *Almost.* I still hadn't forgotten that fat cow comment.

For a moment, they stood there in silence, Lauren crying quietly while Reed acted bored, staring at anything except Lauren, including picking at his nails.

I assume he chose not to pretend any longer and sighed while rolling his eyes. "Right. Well, I have a meeting. Let me know your decision."

Lauren laid a hand on his arm. "You're so cold to me. I give you everything and you won't do this one thing for me."

He pried her hand off his arm and flicked it away with icy precision as he shook his head. "No, I won't, Lauren. You have run your father's company into the ground. It's worthless now. It would not be a good business decision for me to pull it out from this. Let it go."

It appeared she was frozen in shock.

"I'm sure you can find something else to do with your time," he declared.

She glared daggers at him. "You bastard!" When she slapped him, I winced. That had to hurt. He simply spun around to walk away.

I quickly moved the fern back and inched away toward a nearby furniture store, confident he hadn't seen me. Strolling through the large place, I mentally picked out couches, chairs, and dining sets for the time when I would feel confident enough to leave the guesthouse. After several minutes, I glanced out the giant windows, searching for Reed, and noted he wasn't in the vicinity any longer.

With a sigh of relief, I started to leave but saw the restroom and decided to pop in to freshen up. It was when I exited and moved toward the exit that something weird happened though.

"Excuse me, Ma'am," I heard but I paid the voice no attention since it wouldn't be for me and I was running late. Agnes admired punctuality above all things, and she would be furious if I did not make it back to the office on time. I hurried briskly toward the door, my three-inch heels tapping across the tile. I glanced back to find an aggressive sales-woman in hot pursuit. Why?

"No, thank you," I called out over my shoulder, and she still followed. *Really, this was taking a possible sale a bit too far! This was almost harassment!*

I ran out the door without paying attention to anything, crashing straight into Reed. He caught me then looked past my shoulder as the sales lady caught up with me. "Starting a new fashion trend?" he inquired with a lift of his brow.

I had absolutely no idea what he was talking about.

The sales clerk began tugging at my waist. "Your skirt is caught on your waistband," she whispered.

Oh my God! I had scurried through the store with my skirt tucked into the top of my thong panties. I had just mooned the mall! Worse yet, Reed, still holding me, was staring at my naked ass!

I frantically pushed myself away from him and attempted to yank down the offending skirt, as the nervous sales lady tried to help. In my haste, the delicate lace of my panties tore with a rip, dangling around my hip. I froze, praying that without movement, they would stay, but no, the damn things slid down my leg and landed around my feet.

I lifted my knee, ready to grab, but Reed was quicker. He collected them from around my shoe and handed them back to me, where I hastily stuffed the ruined material into my purse. He might have taken a peek at my oohoo, but I refused to think about that right now.

He said absolutely nothing, but his eyes were twinkling with merriment. Of course, my face became as red as a lobster. *Please God, let the ground open up and suck me down.*

I didn't realize I'd said the last part out loud until he laughed.

"No need for that, Miranda, I've seen a few over the years, although, yours is quite lovely."

Forget red, I was glowing now!

"I'll see you at the office, and I'll inform Agnes you were delayed doing some errands for the event." With that, he sauntered away.

I stood there staring at him while people still gawked at me and the saleslady murmured something. I wondered whether or not he would say anything to anyone, then dismissed those thoughts. Reed would never peek and tell… I hoped.

I gathered what was left of my dignity and headed to the lingerie shop to grab some new undies, full coverage granny panties.

Chapter Six

Saturday dawned bright and sunny, and I was fully energized and ready to wish my good friend and her husband all the happiness they deserved as a family. I was going to miss Tessa since she was going away for an entire month to take a relaxing vacation in Europe before bringing her new babies home to the States. Today's party would also be a sort of 'bon voyage' for the two of them, although, it was a girls' only thing.

I dressed in the required black/white attire, pinning my now long red hair—thanks to Sadie's expertise with hair color and extensions—up and away from my face. Chloe, rather than subduing the story behind the children, had decided to not only bring it into the open but to celebrate the sweet heroism of the older black child protecting the younger white child, reminding everyone children don't see color; they simply see a person in need.

I grabbed my black stilettos and the beautifully wrapped music box, heading for my car. "Keys, alarm system, jacket in case it turns colder, purse, present..." I mumbled my list under my breath. "I'm ready!"

Starting the car, I pulled out of the garage and headed to Chloe's townhouse, Tessa would meet me there since she had a few things to do first. Singing along with the radio, I passed the time on the interstate, took the exit I needed to the county road. Chloe lived in the suburbs, sort of. It was actually an old nursery that had gone under, and town-houses have been built in its place. A peaceful wooded oasis in the middle of a cross section of interstate. Chloe loved it.

The first thing I noticed wrong with the car, the chug-ging sound it started making. I looked down at the gas meter. The arrow pushed beyond the red warning. *Where the hell was the warning beep?* Oh yeah, I'd heard it on my way home during the downpour last night. Damn! I knew there was something I'd forgotten! As my car slowed, I maneu-vered it over to the side of the road. Thankfully, it chugged its last chug as I parked and not any sooner.

Glancing down at my striped knee-highs and stilettos, I sighed. My phone indicated no service available on this small sliver of road. I also had no magical button on the dash to call for help, my car was too old. I guessed I was walking to the shower. Getting out of the car, I locked it and started down the road.

It wasn't long before my back hurt and my feet were on

fire. It couldn't be that much further. "I am confident, classy, and a bit sassy. Oh, and an idiot for running out of gas in these heels." I shouted to the trees. I was contemplating whether going barefoot on hot asphalt or following the shade of the trees would be a better option when I heard the hum of a vehicle coming in the opposite direction. I jumped up and down as much as possible in these shoes to flagged it down.

As it approached, I admired the sleek black design. I'd never seen a car like this, which appeared worth a lot of money. The shaded window slid down, and I gaped at the driver. *Fuck me!*

"Having some car trouble?" Reed asked.

Of all the people... Well, there was no hope for it. "Yes, thanks for stopping." I leaned into the interior. "My car is about a mile back that way."

"A mile back? I think I can see it from here."

I looked through the windshield and found the outline of my vehicle. "Well, it felt like I walked a mile," I grumbled. "What are you doing out here?"

"I dropped off a gift for Jerome and Tessa." He stared at me while I thought about the sweet gesture. I snapped back to reality when he huffed, "Well, are you getting in or not?"

"Oh! Oh, yes, thank you." I stepped back, and the door slid open silently. I took a step toward it, or tried to, and wobbled, crashing onto the car seat. My heels were stuck in the hot tar on the side of the road.

"For goodness sakes, take off those damn shoes and get in," he muttered. "You aren't hurt, are you?"

I tried to release my feet from the offending heels without stepping in the tar, but it wasn't easy. Finally, I gave up, stepped onto the gravel and tar, and swiveled my big rear into the seat. I hurriedly stripped off the now tar encrusted socks and threw them outside by the shoes. I was barefoot and mortified, but I was no longer walking. *Thank God I shaved my legs this morning.*

With the push of a button, Reed closed the door. I was ensconced in a small sports car with my boss and trying to think of something to say as he maneuvered the car back onto the road, driving toward the townhouse. "It's a lovely day, isn't it?"

He eyes darted down to my pink painted toes. "Would you say it's a nice day for a stroll?"

He was teasing me and I laughed, feeling a bit more at ease. "Maybe not a stroll, but a drive. This is a lovely car. What kind is it?" I ran my hands along the door. The dashboard looked like a tech lovers' dream—all touchpads and illuminated dials.

"It's a Bugatti prototype. Well, actually, it's a rejected prototype. They just sold the accepted one."

I gaped at him. "The one for 18 million?"

He nodded. "This was my favorite, so I bought it."

"You said rejected?" I glanced around. How could this beauty be a reject?

"Mm, yes." He turned into the entrance of Chloe's subdivision. "It wasn't fast enough. Can only go 245."

"Wow!" I sank back into the buttery soft leather, touched the seat belt. "It's beautifully made."

"I enjoy beautiful things. I'm not all business," he murmured as he slowed the car, stopping in front of Chloe's place.

For some reason, his words brought to mind Lauren. She was beautiful, a perfect match for him. Not some klutzy divorced secretary who showed up barefoot to a baby shower. Oh well. "Thank you for the ride." I tried to get out but had no idea how.

"Just a minute, Miranda." He laid a tanned hand on my arm, and I felt the chemistry all the way to my toes. "I hope you've learned your lesson about the heels and, of course, making sure your car is properly maintained. I'll have it towed and checked for possible trouble. In the future, make sure you heed the warning lights. There's a reason they are there."

I gaped at him. Did he just lecture me on car maintenance? I realized I'd forgotten the gas, but with the rain, and—

I was suddenly furious that he thought I was such an idiot, never mind that I called myself one a few minutes ago. Him saying something was different. "I appreciate your concern, Reed, but I'll take care of my own car. I am a responsible person, despite what you may think." Icicles could have spit from my lips due to my icy tone.

His expression became perplexed. His brow furrowed, and his mouth pressed together momentarily. "I think you're incredibly responsible, Miranda. Otherwise, I wouldn't have given you your position at the company. You simply don't take care of yourself because you're too busy taking care of others."

"How on earth do you know that?" I wasn't letting him off that easily. I was still insulted.

"You noticed Agnes' back hurt and brought her that

godawful smelling herbal heating pad from Sadie. She swears by it now and never goes anywhere without it. You investigated the daycare at the company, talked to Agnes about the complaints from the employees, and found another retired teacher to oversee the whole thing to make everyone happy. You made sure Suzanne had flowers and a comfortable, quiet place to pump milk for her newborn—"

"That just wasn't for Suzanne. It was for the whole company. It was an area no one used."

"You wear ridiculous clothes and silly shoes because your friends picked them for you or told you that's what you needed to be beautiful."

I drew back in anger. "I do not!"

He pointed to my hair and my bare feet. "My guess is Sadie experimented with your hair, and Chloe said you should dress in black and white. She probably told you to wear those suicide heels like she does as well."

"Let me out of this car. My style is none of your business!"

"It's not your style, Miranda, which is the whole point. And it's going to get you hurt. You fell on a sidewalk. That's how you met my brother. You're bleeding from blisters on my car mats, and you're too top heavy to wear heels that high."

"Let me out of this car this instant, and I wouldn't bleed on your precious car any longer, Mr. Michaels. As far as my weight and my style, it's none of your concern. You aren't sleeping with me!" I was tearing up, both furious and hurt

The door slid open suddenly, and I scrambled out, grabbing the present and storming away as dignified as I could in bare feet.

"Miranda!"

I kept walking.

"I mean it. I'll take care of your car and send James to collect you after the shower."

I flipped him off. So much for Reed Michaels and his pompous attitude. If I didn't need the job, I'd quit.

I stepped into the foyer, greeted by my buddies, who sympathized with me over my mishap, brought me chocolate cake and red wine, and made me laugh. I didn't tell them about Reed's lecture. While not totally forgotten, Reed's hurtful words were pushed to the back of my mind as the joy of impending motherhood and friends took me to my happy place.

Once the shower ended, Jerome showed up with a moving van–yes, we needed a van to haul the goodies out– allowing me to ride home with Tessa instead of waiting around for James. I didn't want anything from Reed Michaels.

"You seemed overly upset when you got there today, honey. I got the impression it might be from more than the car situation. Everything OK with Reed?"

"It was terribly embarrassing, Tessa, but nothing new for me, right?" I mumbled, staring out the passenger window.

"I know. He's your boss. You want him to think highly of you."

"No chance of that," I snorted.

Tessa gaped at me, her eyes wide. "Why on earth do you say that?"

I relayed the conversation with Reed. Expecting to hear support, it floored me when she agreed with him. "You think I'm fat, too?"

"Nonsense! That's not what he said!" Tessa pulled into the driveway, hitting the security button. "He was trying to be delicate, Miranda. You're built like a pinup girl. Big boobs and ass. Tottering around on those damn shoes like Chloe doesn't make any sense. He's right."

"What? I'm just supposed to forget what everyone said about being a hot woman with style, and go back to being dull Miranda?" I cried.

Tessa parked the car and turned to me. "Honey, we said find yourself. This," she pointed to my hair," is Sadie. The shoes are Chloe. The tight skirts and stuff are Kimy." She patted my hand. "Be You."

"I'm a klutz. A doormat."

"Stop that! Stop it right now!" Tessa got out of the car, slamming the door as I exited the other side. "You are brave, compassionate, beautiful when you let yourself be the true you, and smarter than most people I've ever met."

She pointed her finger at me. She was really worked up as she came around the car to my side. "You don't think about yourself at all though. You are always last so you don't hurt someone's feelings. Well, screw them. Screw me if I say something you don't like. Let us in, honey. Let us know. Be you in all that fire and glory."

I hugged her hard. She was right. I wasn't being the real me. "I suppose I should apologize to Reed." I jogged to the guesthouse and put my key in the lock, Tessa hot on my heels.

"Why?"

"I sort of flipped him the bird at Chloe's."

"Well, I wished I would have been there for that!" Agnes shouted.

I screamed as she came around the corner from the main house, carrying a large box.

"Here. This is for you. Reed was an ass. How unusual." She smirked. "He's apologizing, which is a first. Take it."

Taking the box from her, I tried to calm my pounding heart as Agnes walked away. "Don't you want to know what's inside?" I called out, noticing the holes in the top of the box and the whining coming from inside. It wasn't light either.

Agnes waved. "I know what's inside. I've been smelling it for half an hour."

I took a sniff as Tessa closed the door to the guesthouse. It didn't smell like cake, that's for sure. I opened the card.

DEAR MIRANDA,

I'M afraid I've hurt your feelings when that was my last intention. I simply wanted you safe. In my error, I behaved less like Prince Charming and more like the fire-breathing dragon. Perhaps he will do a better job of it.

REED

. . .

I UNTIED THE BOW, lifted the lid, and out jumped a German Shepherd puppy. "Oh my! His tag says Prince Charming," I told Tessa. She grabbed the note before the puppy could chew it. Barking with joy, the chubby puppy licked at my face, scratched my arm, and wiggled down to inspect the premises.

"Well, you better get him trained as soon as possible." She slapped her hands together as the puppy lifted a leg to the coffee table. "No! Prince!"

I laughed as it ambled over to Tessa, his expression completely innocent. She put her hands on her hips. "I guess this is what Reed meant when he said he would see to your safety while we were gone."

I peered up. "Why would he say that?"

Tessa picked up the puppy and dropped it into my lap. "Because he likes you, Miranda. Now, it's time for you to decide between the two brothers, personally, my money's on Reed despite that fact he bought you a poop factory. Prince, no!"

Sure enough, my charming Prince was laying claim to his territory in a tried and true tradition.

Chapter Seven

It was the night of the ball. The girls and I had perused shop after shop to find the perfect outfit for the event. I searched for something sexy, but not too showy. My curves and height made it rather difficult. I wanted a great color but nothing too flashy. Sophisticated, classy, but also sassy. We narrowed it down to four choices, but as I stood there debating on them, the saleswoman walked up with "The One".

"It's perfect." The dress was a beautiful charcoal gray, beading down the bodice, off the shoulder, with a deep V inset with lace for modesty. The bottom came to an inverted V to highlight my waist and camouflage my larger hips. It was almost like it was made for me. The small train in the back gave me a bit of trepidation, but I could be careful and not klutzy just this once…I hoped. It was the most beautiful dress I'd ever seen.

"Would you like to try it on?"

"Definitely!" Tessa answered before I could open my mouth.

I knew this was it as soon as I put it on, and the girls agreed.

"Oh my," Sadie gasped. "You're right. This is the one. It even brings out the red highlights in your hair."

Thankfully, I had returned to my honey blonde with subtle copper highlights, minus the extensions.

Tessa looked like she was going to cry.

"Definitely the one," Chloe smiled.

Kimy, ever practical, stated the obvious, "We have to find shoes that will work with it so you don't trip on the train and fall on your face." She had a twinkle in her eyes, and I could tell she liked the dress as well.

I bought the dress and asked about shoes and purchased a pair of strappy sandals in the same charcoal grey with a four-inch heel—thankfully, not too high, or not as high as Chloe made me wear. My feet were gonna kill me, but they were perfect.

On the advice of Tessa, we decided to make ourselves beautiful. And I was happy every one of my friends had been invited. Jerome and Reed were good friends, Ritter and Chloe knew each other through acquaintances, Kimy had done business with Reed, and she took Sadie as her plus one just for fun. We did the works–beautiful hair quaffed, makeup done professionally, and a body exfoliation with soothing lotions and light massage. When I peered into the mirror, I didn't recognize myself. The ladies were equally impressive.

"Wow," Kimy said. "We rock!"

Sadie looked a little uncomfortable in the evening wear, but I was sure she could manage.

Tessa, stunning as always in her lavender chiffon dress, took command as usual, "All right ladies, we are gorgeous. We know how to behave. Let's do this thing."

We headed toward the elegant stairs of Tessa's mansion, branching out to greet the men.

Ritter very graciously had asked me to be his plus one at the function. There had been a bit of awkwardness since Reed was at my desk at the time. "Please, feel free to go with my brother. I'm sure he'll behave himself while he's there," he stated with a warning glance at Ritter.

"Of course, dear brother. Why would I not? I 've been to enough of these stuffy, boring parties. I plan to enjoy being with someone who isn't quite so stiff."

I could feel the underlying tensions between the two, but I didn't quite understand why.

When I came down the stairs, trying desperately not to trip on my gown, I heard the wolf whistle. Ritter was at the bottom looking charming as always in his Armani tuxedo. "I am the luckiest man alive. I will have the most beautiful woman at my side." He kissed my cheek.

"Thank you, Sir. You look very dashing yourself.

He nodded in agreement and off we went. I felt like Cinderella at the ball, although, I'm pretty sure the pumpkin wasn't a Maserati, and Cinderella didn't get the shit scared out of her on the way with the coachman's erratic driving.

We arrived, and I excused myself to mingle. After making several introductions, I left to check on the dinner arrangements, ensuring everything was prepared. Agnes stood in the kitchen, her sturdy frame in a lovely black pantsuit, always sensible shoes on her feet, and she was barking orders as usual.

She seemed surprised when she noticed me but quickly smiled and said, "You look lovely, dear.

"You do, too."

"Yes, but I'm afraid I would feel more comfortable in my office attire."

"This is a bit much for me as well."

"You'll get used to it," she snickered and smacked me on the back, probably checking to see if I would fall over in my shoes. "Oh dear, what do you have on your feet?" She glared down at my slim stilettos, shaking her head. "Well, there's no help for it now. Try not to slip." *Pragmatic as usual.* I asked if there was anything I could do, but she turned me away, "No thanks. I know how to handle anything that crops up. You did an excellent job."

"I'll remember you saying that 'til my dying day," I teased her.

"There's no need for such nonsense," she huffed. "You deserve the praise and the credit." She took the tray of empty glasses from a passing waiter.

"Well, Suzanne's back and this is finished. I'm not exactly sure where I'm going next within the corporation." I hoped that was subtle enough. Who knew, maybe she'd heard something about what would happen to me.

"Reed didn't tell you? You're going to be training with

me. I'm retiring at the end of the year, and you will be my replacement." She continued, "I'll occasionally step in here and there, but I think you'll do a bang-up job. You're not so young as to be frivolous. You're not so old as to worry about things like trying to snare Reed. You seem to know what you're doing, have good communication skills, and you don't bore people with stupid chatter and drama. Thank God. I think you're exactly what Reed needs."

"Thank you." I wasn't sure working with Reed day in and day out was such a good idea. My feelings for him were confusing, to say the least. Once again, I lost myself in my thoughts before I remembered Agnes, who was staring at me strangely. *Did I say that out loud?*

She winked at me. "Given what's going to be happening in the next few months, I'll be glad to hand over the reins."

"I don't understand."

"Maybe you're not as sharp as I thought you were. Come here." She shoved me out of the kitchen and into an alcove near a coat rack. "Reed is in the fight of his life for the company. The board of directors is iffy on his continued status within. It's ridiculous, of course. Reed IS Michaels Group. I'm not certain how the questions or the concerns came about. Everyone knows that he's the man for the job, not Ritter.

"Ritter?"

Agnes nodded. "Yes, he's making a bid for the company president position. He's got a few followers, but some who are backing him are tried and true conservatives. I have no idea why they are supporting him at all." Her eyes suddenly grew wide. "You came with him, didn't you? Perhaps I've said too much."

She tried to walk away, but I grabbed her hand. "We're simply friends. I don't understand. I knew they had a sibling rivalry, but a takeover?" I was appalled. Reed worked damn hard to keep this corporation successful. As far as I could tell, Ritter simply entertained the clients.

"Oh, I doubt it'll go through." She leaned in. "What kind of board of directors replaces a perfectly competent head with a flamboyant playboy? He has no more business running the company than…well…my cat!" she harrumphed.

"I knew the quarterly projections were down this year."

"Reed might not be the man causing the issues. Everyone knows he's great with figures, but he does lack certain social panache." She gestured to the dance floor where he was standing somewhat stiffly nodding to someone and appearing bored. Next to him, the ever-present Lauren did all the talking, so I assume they patched up their differences. Her animated smile seemed rather forced, but what the hell did I know?

"All those social niceties that Ritter possesses are fine, but I would think it's Reed's business acumen is what keeps the board of directors happy."

"You'd think so," Agnes groused. She took another sip of her champagne. "But we have some new board members. Some of the retired ones have given their shares to their children, and Ritter is more fun, which caters to them. This isn't a fun spot. This is a corporation which employs thousands of people all over the world. If Ritter succeeds, I fear a collapse."

"I had no idea, Agnes. I'm sorry."

She patted my hand. "Just goes to show, you don't have time for office gossip. You're a good egg, Miranda. Don't let Ritter charm you into foolishness."

"I understand perfectly Ritter's fun is not for me. I need a milder sort of entertainment."

"No, you need someone who will be there for the long haul, and you deserve someone as a wonderful as you are."

I hugged her. "You taught me so much. Thank you."

"Nonsense!" She patted my shoulder. "Don't start weeping, honey, or you'll ruin your pretty face. Come on, let's go mingle and make sure Reed stays the president of the corporation." She turned back when I stumbled and snapped, "Get rid of those ridiculous heels you wear. And if I find out you said anything in Ritter about this, you're dead to me."

I nodded frantically. Agnes really could be quite terrifying.

I danced with several of the gentlemen on the board and talked to the ladies of the board in the powder room. I tried my darnedest to make sure everyone understood Reed's business acumen was without parallel. It was the least I could do since he had been so kind to me.

I chatted with Tessa, commiserated with Chloe over aching feet, watched as Kimy tried to ward off several advances, and look on as Sadie invaded the dance floor with her own brand of the waltz.

Lauren was in her element, dancing with one partner

after another. She was extremely confident. Actually, I wished I could stand to walk in these damn heels like she does. I couldn't wait to kick them off.

"You did a great job, Miranda. I couldn't have asked for a more elegant social gathering. Thank you," Reed stated rather stiffly.

"Thank you. I'm glad it turned out well."

"Agnes mentioned that she told you about your new position in the company."

"She told me."

"I prefer you to keep it quiet until after the vote from the board next month. They don't know you, and although you seem charming and organized, I don't want anything to ruin my chances to retain the company.

"I completely understand, Reed. I'm sorry to hear you have been put in this position. You are the heart and soul of Michaels Group."

"I wasn't aware you were kept in the dark about the impending board of directors meeting or the hostile takeover by Ritter."

"No, I'm afraid it wasn't informed. I'm sorry, if I had known, I would have never accepted his invitation."

"Why?" Reed asked.

"Because it's disloyal to you!"

He stared at me with those intense dark eyes. "You know Ritter's reputation. You're not going to change that."

I wasn't sure what he was talking about.

"He's a playboy, Miranda. He doesn't actually desire you personally. He wants the appearance you bring. That's all, and if you make him look at least semi-conservative and responsible, he will use it to his advantage and discard you when he's through. It's his modus operandi.

Yes, Reed definitely needed a class on social niceties and tact. "I know Ritter isn't the relationship kind, Reed."

"And what about you, Miranda? Why are you still even seeing him? I don't believe for a minute he desires you for you. If he wanted arm candy, he could go for any number of nubile young things. He wants you for something else."

That hurt–I wasn't good enough for a real relationship with one of the Michaels brothers. That was what Reed implied. I swallowed my pride and tried not to tear up. "I'm well aware of that, Reed. I'm also aware of how you feel about my relationship with Ritter. There's no need to be so blunt. I know I'm not the type of woman your titan family would even consider as a mate."

He frowned at me.

I spoke through clenched teeth, "I will reiterate once again that we are only friends, and you can take your damn opinion and shove it up your tight ass." There was nothing more to be said, therefore, I headed to the stairs in order to leave. I had more than likely lost my job with my outburst.

Once again, my inner "Grace" possessed me. As I kicked out my foot to take the first step, I flipped head over heels down the long flight, grabbing for the railing but only catching air. I tumbled, hitting my head, bruising my eye. Pain exploded on my side as I finally stopped on the landing, my gray dress pooled around my hips. I supposed I should be thankful this time my panties held.

The sound of rushing feet behind me, as well as several gasps, had me craning my neck to see who witnessed my debacle–practically everyone. I valiantly tried to get to my feet and exit with as much dignity as possible, but my ankle wasn't having it. Pain shot straight through to my heart, and I collapsed again, no longer able to contain the tears.

"Let me see." Reed's gentle voice came from beside me.

Of all people, he was the last person I wanted to help me. "No, leave me alone." I jerked away, my bodice ripping then, and out plops my boob. *Great, could this get any more humiliating?*

I jerked my head back to gape up at Reed, only to find him staring at my right nipple, and I immediately covered myself.

That seemed to knock him out of his stupor. "Stop being stubborn, woman, and let me examine at your ankle."

He made no attempt to help me rectify my dress, and I quickly pulled the shoulder strap back up. Closing my eyes, I wished for all of them to go away.

"Is she all right?" I heard Agnes' worried voice. "I told her not to wear those stupid shoes."

"Get me some ice, Agnes, and then call James. I want him up here to take her down and home."

I peered around Reed and saw her disappearing into the crowd as Tessa took her place.

"Oh, honey." She brushed my hair back where it had fallen from its elegant chignon.

"I just hit my face, and hurt my ankle," I mumbled. I also didn't mention the pain in my side. "I'll be fine, well, except for my dignity."

Kimy appeared, looked down briefly, and then waved to

the crowd. "OK, people, nothing to see here. Nothing to see. Go on. A little twisted ankle. Enjoy the festivities."

I was never so grateful for her brusque manner as when everyone began to disperse.

I wiped my tears only to see Reed's angry visage. "Why do you insist on wearing these stupid shoes? You are going to kill yourself! Do you realize you could have broken your neck? Fallen over the edge of the railing? My God, isn't that how you met Ritter, tripping over in heels landing in his lap?" He took a breath and continued while I simply gaped at him, "Look at your foot!" He gently cradled my ankle in his large hand, spreading his fingers from my toe to my heel. "I can span it with my fingers. What size are you? A six?"

I glared at him. He glared back until I conceded. "Yes," I murmured.

"Then don't be an idiot! You cannot wear five-inch heels when your foot isn't even half that size. You're constantly on the balls of your feet. You're not exactly a slim woman."

Oh, how dare he bring that up now!

He continued his tirade, "How do you expect to walk in these things? That's why you're always falling! You're trying to balance all this," he waved at my body, "on toothpicks!"

Well, that tears it! "I appreciate your assistance, but my friends can help me from here, and you don't have to fire me because I quit."

Reed's mouth dropped open, and then he frowned. "Don't be ridiculous. You need health care, especially if you're going to be continually falling because you won't listen to reason."

He stood up as a large man approached. "James take

her home, make sure she gets in bed." The man immediately bent down to carry me. "Agnes, go with her."

"No! Agnes has to stay here in case something happens at the party."

"I don't give a damn about the party!" he snapped.

"My dear," Agnes smiled kindly, "I think something has already happened at the party."

I shook my head as James effortlessly lifted me into his arms. Luckily, Sadie approached at that precise moment.

"I will take care of her. I'm finished here." She mumbled some sort of gibberish chant and bowed.

Reed seemed skeptical, but he gave in. "All right then." He turned to Kimy. "Unless you think she needs to go to the to the hospital?" He answered his own question. "Yes, let's take her to the hospital."

"Absolutely not! It's a sprained ankle. I'll be fine with some ice and Motrin."

Sadie studied my swelling appendage closely, poking at it. "I don't think it's broken, just a bad sprain. Now the cut on your head…" She spit on her thumb and used it to wipe away the blood as Reed grimaced in disgust. "Nope, she's OK there, too. Just a surface cut. Head injuries, even minor ones, bleed like a stuck pig."

"You are going to the hospital," Reed announced.

I grabbed his jacket. "No, it's fine. Please," I beseeched him. I just wanted to go home and for this horrible ordeal to end.

He studied me for a moment, eventually sighing as he shook his head. "As you wish." He nodded to James.

We started off, Sadie clucking behind me holding my

shoe. I glanced over James' shoulder, up the stairs, and sought out Reed. He was easily found, tall and handsome, looking down at me, Lauren at his side. She kissed him on the cheek, smirking at me. I dropped my gaze.

Exiting the hotel, we made an odd little group. The large, silent black man carrying a barefoot woman in a ball-gown with a redhead in a caftan sprinkling something in front of us as we walked while she hummed a tune. It was, by all appearances, just a somewhat typical night for Miranda the Klutz...minus the whole ball gown thing.

THE NEXT EVENING, I was comfortably ensconced on my sofa, foot bandaged and propped up when someone knocked at the door. "Come in," I called out, taking a sip of the tea Sadie had made and insisted I drink three times a day. I shuddered. It was godawful, but I didn't want to hurt her feelings.

"It's me, and I brought visitors and gifts," Tessa announced,

I glanced up to see her arms full of flowers and Agnes walking calmly behind her carrying some boxes. "Oh, Agnes, I'm so glad to see you. I feel terrible about leaving the clean-up to you."

She set the gifts down on the table and claimed the chair by the fireplace. "Everything was handled by the catering crew. You did an excellent job making sure the party was a success, as well as the clean-up, and you know that, so stop fishing for compliments."

I laughed out loud. I loved her brand of charm.

Tessa set the large vase of flowers on the coffee table and handed me the card. "I'm going to get us some lemonade." She marched into the small kitchen next to my living room.

I could hear her puttering around muttering to herself as I opened the card to find the flowers were from Agnes. "You didn't have to do that." I grinned at her.

"Nonsense," she said. "It's the least I could do. You worked hard and were injured in the line of duty." The twinkle in her eye belied her brisk tone.

She handed me a small box. "These are from Ritter," she stated with a frown. "Perhaps there's an explanation as to where he was when you fell."

"Don't be like that, Agnes. I said I'm sure there was a good explanation as to why…well, there probably isn't a good explanation, or at least, one I want to hear," I admitted. "Let's leave it. Besides, we're only friends. I've already made that perfectly clear." I pulled the ribbon, noting the famous pale blue box. Inside, a small note that read,

MY DEAREST MIRANDA,

MY DEEPEST APOLOGIES for not being there at your time of need. Perhaps I can make it up to you in some small way with this token.

YOURS, Ritter

. . .

"WELL?" Agnes demanded.

I shook my head. And took out the small velvet box, opening it to reveal two large diamond stud earrings. "Oh my! These are beautiful."

Agnes got up and peeked over my shoulder. "Hmm, Tiffany's. At least three carats. That's a nice makeup gift, but where was he?"

"I have no idea." I pulled the beautiful earrings from the box and removed my simple hoops. I reverently placed the diamonds in my ears. Agnes, ever efficient, had her compact open and ready for me to view them.

"They look good on you," she stated, "Now where was he?"

Exasperated, I narrowed my eyes. "I have no idea, but I did make it home safe and sound. My ankle isn't broken, it simply requires a few days of rest. Ritter and I are only friends."

"So, what's in the other box?" I peered at my earrings again, trying to take her mind off of it.

"I know what you're doing, but here, this is from Reed."

I eagerly grabbed the box, not quite sure why my heart skipped a beat. The card on top simply read, *Get Well Soon* but as I opened it, Reed's scrawl jumped out at me. No 'dearest' sadly, but...

MIRANDA, if I see you wearing anything other than these I WILL fire you on the spot–Reed.

. . .

OPENING THE BOX, I laughed. A new pair of sneakers in my exact size sat nestled among the tissue paper. Stuffed inside were six pairs of frilly socks with another note.

I KNOW how you like to make a fashion statement.

I BLUSHED crimson at the reminder of Reed catching me with my panties down…literally.

Agnes, always observant, noticed immediately. "So, what has you going red? You gushed over Ritter's gift, and yet, you've fallen silent and blushing with Reeds."

I turned even redder. She cackled in glee right as Tessa came through the door. "Oh, those earrings! Wow! They catch the sunlight! Are those from Reed?"

"No, from Ritter. These," I held up the shoes, "are from Reed."

"Of course. Ritter will go with diamonds, and Reed will give you just what you need."

"Truer words were never spoken," Agnes stated, staring directly at me.

I shook my head. "One is my boss, the other my friend, and I have enough on my plate as it is. Romance is not in the picture."

Agnes got up, kissed me on the forehead and patted my shoulder. "I'm off, and as far as romance goes, it may not be in the picture for you, dear, but it's on the mind of at least one of these men. I'll see you at the office next week."

I waved goodbye as she walked out the door, chuckling to herself.

Tessa handed me a glass of lemonade. "I don't suppose I'll ever figure Agnes out. She is a wonder unto herself."

She sat back comfortably in the chair Agnes had vacated. "What was all that about romance? What are you going to do about Reed?"

I lowered my eyes to the shoes. *What indeed!*

Chapter Eight

After a week off, I was more than ready to get back to work. Agnes greeted me warmly, Ritter declared I looked even more radiant after my rest, and Reed simply nodded after dropping his gaze to make sure I wore his gift. Nothing was ever mentioned about my quitting comment.

Agnes called me into Reed's office around mid-morning to discuss the current daycare situation. "I told Reed some of the ideas you had, and he would like to put you in charge of revamping not only the daycare floor but the curriculum as well. I believe all but two of the staff are certified teachers in elementary education. We can offer to subsidize the degree programs if the other two would like to receive their certification."

Reed spoke up, "I want everyone involved with the children to be licensed to teach, background checks, proper insurance, CPR certified, whatever else you can think of. We should have top-notch daycare for our employees. There's absolutely no reason not to. It will cost us less in the long run if we have happier employees, plus they should have fewer days off work."

My fingers flew across the notepad. I was old school. I needed a pad and paper like the younger staff needed their tablets. "Would you like me to look over the nutritional value of the lunches and snacks?"

"When I said everything, I meant everything. If there's a hole in the system, you need to find it and plug it. Better safe than sorry, don't you agree?"

I smiled. "Absolutely. Anything else?"

Reed sat back in his chair. "Not at the moment. Agnes and I still have a few things to discuss."

"I guess you best get to it," Agnes stated. I got up to leave.

"Oh, and Miranda?" Reed stopped me. "While you're working with the daycare, it's business casual. I'm sure you can find something to go with your shoes."

I look down at my pencil skirt and frilly blouse complete with my tennis shoes and laughed. "Yes, Sir!" I gave him a smart salute.

Agnes harrumphed, but he smiled. "Carry on."

I left the room light-hearted, anxious to get started on my new project, my heart fluttering at the warmer reception I got from Reed.

As the weeks went on, I poured over nutritional programs, the latest in playground equipment, safety classes for all new employees, background checks on teachers and staff. I listened to suggestions, complaints, concerns, as well as positive ideas, thoughts on the program itself, and new diversity programs to meet the needs of the foreign staff here for long-term projects.

I soon realized I was going to need help, so I approached Reed as he was leaving for the day. Running for the elevator as he stepped on, I panted out, "Reed, please wait a moment."

He held the door, and I stepped in. "Something I can help you with, Miranda?"

"I have two questions. Do you think it would be possible for me to get some part-time help with the correlation of the information and resources I have in order to make these informed decisions and present them to the committee?"

"Of course that's no problem take it up with HR in the morning. What else?"

I noticed he seemed to be a bit irritated, so I rushed on, "The second thing...it came to my attention, since you gave me Prince, that a pet-friendly atmosphere," he looked at me sharply, "Hear me out. People who may worry about their animals to feel more comfortable..." I lost my nerve. He was frowning intently.

"Yes?" he prompted me to go on.

"If we had a place, an area, say this side yard that isn't being used. It's simply a grassy knoll."

"It's green space," he muttered.

"I understand that, but can't we use that 'green space'," I used air quotes, "and perhaps facilitate that area next to it.

"The warehouse?" he sputtered.

"It's not really a warehouse, Reed. It's simply a place to store stuff."

The elevator stopped, but he made no move to leave. "I know which one you mean."

"It could house a doggy daycare."

"You want people to be able to bring their dogs to work."

"I have to pay for mine to be watched during the day. Why not offer it is one of the perks?" I cajoled.

"Wouldn't we be discriminating–only dogs?" He smirked.

"We could have kitty camps, too."

"Kitty camps," he mumbled under his breath. "What's next snake soirees?"

"We could have a reptile section, but we'll see how it goes."

He shook his head, but his eyes were dancing. "Miranda, whatever you think."

"I think yes!" I clapped, barely restraining myself from giving him a hug. "Thank you!"

"You're in charge of morale."

"I am?"

"You are now. Is there anything else?"

"Oh, no, sorry to bother you. We've been very busy. I haven't had a chance to really talk. I should have made an appointment."

"That's not the problem, Miranda." He stepped out into the main lobby.

"What's the main problem?" I called out, thinking he had been so generous with my idea, that I'd help him if I could.

He turned and looked at me. "You." He winked and took off through the crowd.

I could feel my face go up in flames. George, the security guard, was cackling next to me. *Did that mean he…oh, he's such a mystery!* I hit the button back to the top floor and pondered why on earth a man like Reed Michaels would be bothered by me, grinning the whole way.

Over the next few days, those thoughts were still in the back of my mind as I met the girls for what had become our weekly, instead of monthly, get-togethers. At an elite restaurant near the Chicago lakefront, we settled in with drinks, and I opened the conversation. "What's been happening ladies?"

Kimy shrugged. "Not much. Might have to find a new job. I'm getting really tired of doing the same old thing over and over again. I think I'd really like to travel more."

"You work for a travel agency, why don't you just take on more travel jobs?" Tessa asked.

"It's not so much that as much as I'd like to be my own boss, do my own thing."

Chloe chimed in, "You want to start your own agency?"

"Maybe? It's more like, I don't know, I've got the blog and everything, and it's really doing well, but I need to get out more. I can't write about where I went for work or what I thought was good or bad. Plus, there are some places they don't want to take me to, and so I put them in the blog. I think they're good. Not everybody wants that whole cookie cutter touristy experience. They want to go off the grid."

"Oh, that would be an awesome name!" Sadie exclaimed.

"It is the name of my blog, Sadie. If you ever read it, you'd know."

"I read that first piece, and you were talking about hunting lions. You know how I feel about that."

"We all know, Sadie," I said.

"What would you do for staff? You have to have someone reliable, someone who could have your back. Do you have somebody in your office now, an assistant or whatever, you would like to take with you?" Tessa asked.

"No, she's aiming for my job so I wouldn't trust her as far as I could throw her. I kind of thought that you might like it." She shifted her gaze to Chloe.

"Me? Why me?" Chloe asked.

Kimy shrugged. "Well, we get along. You don't bore me to death, and I don't think I make you cringe too often. I know I could trust you. You know all about computers and all about the business side of things."

"Uh—" Chloe tried and failed to interrupt.

"There are wonderful perks—good insurance, you could help me write the blog if you'd like, have a piece in it yourself, and maybe do some traveling."

"But I'm an accountant," Chloe reminded her.

"Exactly. You could take care of all my expenses as I go on my merry way. That sounds like a headache, but a fun headache," Kimy deadpanned.

I said, "Think of it, Chloe. You're unattached, you're ready to see the world, you never know, you may be scooped up by some Saudi prince."

"I don't think so," Chloe snickered. "I've got my sights set on a cowboy, and somehow, I don't think we're going to be going to Texas."

"Dude ranches," Kimy interjected. "We could go for some of those, not necessarily couple type things, but we could go for the single nights."

"Let me think about it. I won't say I'm not in," Chloe sort of relented.

"Great! We'll talk more later." Kimy gave a rare smile. "Now I feel like some meat."

Sadie grimaced. "You are disgusting."

We put in our order, and I turned to Tessa, "What's new in the life of you and Jerome?"

"You know how Jerome has decided he'd like to run for office?"

We nodded.

"It seems…he'd like to run for mayor."

"The mayor?"

"Yes, he wants to run the city."

"He's been an alderman and had pages. He's contributed to several things, made great strides through the law offices for charities and organizations in the area."

"What do you think about it?" Chloe asked.

Sadie grabbed Tessa's hand. "She thinks it's scary out there."

Tessa snatched her hand away. "I'm not afraid."

Kimy snorted. "You are terrified, but he's the right guy to do it."

Tessa took a drink of her martini. "I realize he's the guy to do it, and I know he should do it, but the selfish part of me feels like Chicago is Gotham City or something, and he's trying to be Batman and save it. One day some weird criminal is going to take a shot at him. I don't know what I'd do without him." Tessa cried into her napkin.

Sadie hugged her.

"We all understand; me probably most of all," Kimy spoke softly, "But I'll tell you from experience, Tessa, if we stop doing what we love out of fear of what could happen, then we're not really living. If he really feels he wants to do this, you need to be brave for him and let him do it because he would do the same for you."

Tessa swiped at her tears. "I know, and that's why he's going to be announcing his bid for mayor next month."

Chloe squealed, "That's fantastic!"

"Hell yeah!" Kimy confirmed. "Can we raise a glass to Jerome."

We all raised them up.

"May he stay safe," said Chloe.

"May he do what's right," added Kimy.

"May he always be a force for change," I stated.

"And may good karma follow him," Sadie murmured.

"And may I be brave," Tessa declared.

We clinked our glasses together.

"You don't have to be brave all the time, Tessa. We will be brave with you," Sadie reminded her.

I nodded through my tears. This is why I loved these gals. No matter what, we were in it together.

"So, what about you, Sadie? Anything new in the crystal business," Never wanting to be the center of attention, Tessa switched the subject as the waiter arrived with our meals.

"I've decided to expand into essential oils along with being a Reiki master, my own psychic abilities, and adding the new shaman who has been coming to my shop. He and I have decided it would be a wonderful way to partner together for wellness."

Chloe looked up from her pasta. "I'm still doing your books right?"

"Oh, absolutely!" Sadie nodded. "In fact, I'll need Jerome, if he has time, to draft up a new contract. My partners said—"

"Woah, woah, woah..." Kimy interrupted. "Nobody goes anywhere with partnerships until we check them out. You know that, Sadie."

"I'm not being shafted like last time," Sadie retorted.

"Then let me check him out."

"OK, I don't know why I bother telling you anything. I'm not an imbecile." She looked as if she was about to cry.

Tessa grabbed her hand. "No, you're not, honey. You are one of the most wonderful, compassionate, and giving people who have ever graced this earth, and it's our job to take care of you because you take care of so many."

Sadie blushed. "I guess it wouldn't hurt to have your brother look into it."

Kimy's brother, an FBI agent, was called upon on occasion. Unfortunately, he and Sadie didn't exactly have a great rapport. He thought she was a crystal waving wacko, and her words were: he's a psychopathic gun-toting gorilla. Personally, I thought she doth protest too much!

We decided on cheesecake for dessert, and when it arrived, I felt all eyes on me. With a sly grin, Chloe broached the subject apparently on all their minds. "You seem to have survived the ball fiasco, Cinderella."

"I heard you got some presents." Kimy winked.

"Oh, yes, I got these earrings from Ritter."

"They are lovely." Chloe admired them.

Kimy even snorted, "Nice rocks," but Sadie was rather quiet for once.

"Tell them what else you got, Miranda." Tessa grinned over her coffee cup.

"Reed gave me a German Shepherd puppy called Prince Charming and a pair of tennis shoes to wear at work. I'm working on the new daycare center for the main office."

Tess snorted delicately. "That's not why he gave them to you."

"I'd like to put my unfortunate fall behind me, thank you very much," I groused.

Sadie smiled and grabbed my hand. "You, my dear, are being courted, but one wonders which brother she will choose."

I pulled my hand away. "Neither. One is my boss, the other is a friend. I know too much about Ritter to ever think he'd be my type."

"Thank God for that," mumbled Kimy under her

breath. "I was afraid I was gonna have to talk to you about him. I've heard some things."

"What things?" I demanded

"That his brother has gotten him out of trouble more times than I can count."

"Well, you're not the accountant," Sadie chirped.

"The ball was full of people commenting on the number of women Ritter has had. In addition, the deals that have gone wrong, the slightly less than legal way he sometimes does business, and when he gets caught, Reed always has to find a way to get him out."

"I'm sure it's becoming quite wearing," Tessa nodded. "I don't mean to sound harsh, Miranda, but I set you up thinking that you would have a good time. I didn't know that he would…" She paused, glancing down at her glass.

That he would be truly interested in me? I thought angrily. "I understand what you're saying, Tessa. I'm not his type. I'm well aware. Everyone has informed me of that, including Reed." I ate a huge bite of cheesecake–I could work it off tomorrow.

"Miranda, you know that's not what we meant. We meant that…" Tessa paused again, seeking guidance from Chloe.

She took up the mantle. "What she's trying to say is, he was fine to, you know, get your feet wet, but he's not the permanent kind. Honey, you deserve better."

"Better than a millionaire?" I scoffed, "And a gorgeous one at that?"

"Yes," Sadie said softly. She met my eyes with a big smile

on her face. "You don't deserve the millionaire, you deserve the billionaire."

I put down my fork. "I don't have any billionaires on my radar at all." All this talk of my sex life was depressing, but I soldiered on so they could get the complete picture. "You know what I do have? Let me sum up a few of the dates I've been on, the ones through those dating services you guys suggested."

I held up one finger. "There was Jonathan. Jonathan, the lawyer, who looked me up and down like I was a piece of meat and declared he liked my ass but my waist could be a little smaller, and by the end of the evening, he was so inebriated I had to call him a cab."

I lifted another finger. "Then there was Bruce, who is a former Air Force pilot. He informed me I was lovely and asked if would I be interested in perhaps taking this to the next level after one date. I asked, 'What level?' He smiled, pulled out his phone, and showed a picture of him amidst two other lovely ladies naked on the bed. They needed an older third to play out 'Mommy' fantasies."

Finger number three. "Jesus! You know the chakra salesman, Sadie?"

"He wasn't a chakra salesman," she retorted. "He sold crystals to help align your chakra."

"Align my chakra? Oh my God! I met him at a Moroccan restaurant. By the time we were finished with dinner, he was sweating profusely, smelled like curry, and had the audacity to tell me to pay for the check as he was a modern man."

"I bet chakra salesmen don't make big money," Chloe teased, managing to keep a straight face.

"Ha-ha, very funny! Should I go on?"

Tessa chortled. "Please do. I haven't had this much fun in a while."

I narrowed my eyes at her. "Very well. Who else did you set me up with? Our Live Time, which is supposedly a site to meet upper-class matches. Yeah. Whatever. For a match? I'm 5 foot 4. The man was shorter than me. Yes, he made a lot of money. I knew that because it was all he talked about, and then he asked if he could try on my shoes!"

Kimy snickered.

"Oh no, you don't get to laugh because you set me up with Bobo the bondage man," I snapped.

"The what?" Chloe exclaimed, but Kimy waved it away.

Shrugging, Kimy said, "So? He was into rope craft. It doesn't mean you had to be."

"Kimy, he took me to a dungeon, a private one, where everyone was naked and on display, there were a variety of implements I had no idea even existed. And don't get me started on what was considered furniture," I declared.

"Did you have a good time?" Kimy asked.

"No, I didn't even make it past the lobby. He took off his clothes in the lobby, and I walked out the door."

Everyone laughed, and I couldn't help it, I did, too. "You never know what to ask on these dating sites. I assumed it would be dinner and drinks," I sighed when I caught my breath.

Sadie giggled. "Dinner, drinks, ropes, and chains."

Chloe added, "Whips and canes."

"Slap and tickle," Tessa whispered.

"Clamps for nipples," Kimy finished the rhyme.

We once again erupted into laughter, so much so, that we were getting looks from the other patrons.

"Who's your next dating adventure?" Tessa inquired.

"I think I'm going to give it a rest for a bit. I'm not sure I can put up with anyone else. Besides, this dinner date then sex lifestyle has me at a loss. You know Rat Bastard was my first and only lover."

"Calling him a lover is an insult to every lover out there. He's like a terrible nurse with a dull syringe. He barely gets you ready for it, shoves the needle in, pumps you full of something you'd rather not have, and then slaps a band-aid on to call it aftercare."

"Oh God! I just got a picture of him in a nurse's uniform! I need another drink! No, I need to concentrate on me. My sexual experiences can wait. I don't see why sex is such a big deal to me, but it is. It's not just an activity. I have to have a real connection, which for me, means a relationship. I don't want sex to simply happen because it's expected or there's chemistry."

Kimy shrugged. "Sometimes you need a release, though. Do you have something for that?"

"KIMY!" Tessa practically shouted.

"I know how to take care of business, Kimy. However, the before and after if I decide to take a lover has me worried. I'm at the point I don't think I want to try. Ritter is a nice man, but he's not going to be a sexual connection. Besides, I have the feeling if he really desired me, he would have made more of a play by now."

Chloe nodded. "I agree. You're actually the longest relationship he's had with a woman, according to his assistant. We take Krav together. She thought the earrings were your goodbye gift instead of a get well."

"I'm constantly amazed at the amount of gossip in that place."

"It's everywhere, honey, not just at Michael's. But there is something I've tried to find the right time to tell you," Chloe said, taking my hand in hers. "The reason they couldn't find Ritter when you were injured at the ball was that he wasn't there. Apparently, he and another woman were seen leaving together about the time you fell."

Sadie patted my other hand. "Don't discount the billionaire I saw in your future."

"Sadie, I'm closing in on fifty, I'm overweight, my hair—"

"Your hair is lovely now," she interrupted as the other girls rolled their eyes. This time it was a burnished copper, much subtler but still not quite me. I'd refused the orange byzantine caftan she wanted me to wear tonight.

"Yes, it is, and it brings out my green eyes, but like I told Tessa the other day, before I concentrate on anybody else, I really need to find the real me"

"Yes," Chloe stated, "She told us you weren't really ready for Randi.

"I'm not. I'm Miranda, and I'm OK with that."

"Want another drink?" Kimy snickered. "That might bring out the Randi in you."

"No, she doesn't," Tessa put her foot down. "She gets into enough trouble sober."

"What trouble? I'm perfectly fine," I spoke up for myself.

"As long as you're wearing the tennis shoes," Chloe retorted.

"Ha-ha! I think they were a very nice gift," I snorted.

"Yes," Chloe agreed, "They were very thoughtful. Now, those diamonds, on the other hand, they were an awesome gift."

Tessa grinned. "But the dog–the dog is what puts it over the top because while one glitters and shines, the other protects and keeps you safe."

"One wishes to simply show you off. The other wishes to show you how precious you truly are. I rest my case," Sadie argued her point in s soft voice. "It's true, all that glitters is not gold."

Chloe made a face. "We're voting Reed? I liked Ritter. He isn't as stuffy."

"What are you talking about?" I had a nagging suspicion they were up to something.

"We're talking your billionaires, darling," Tessa stated matter of factly.

"Oh no!" I waved my hand in the negative.

"Oh yes!" they declared in unison.

"He likes you; he gave you a puppy." Sadie sighed.

"If I'm not Ritter's type, I'm definitely not Reed's type, and did you forget about Lauren?" I shook my head. "Definitely not. I'm not going to romance Reed."

"He'll be glad to hear that. Frankly, so am I," Lauren approached our table.

I plastered on a smile. "Hello, Lauren. How nice to see you again. We were just chatting."

"Yes," she smirked. "About Reed. He's quite a subject, but I'm sure you have other things to talk about other than your boss, Melinda."

I knew she purposely messed up my name. Kimy started to get up, but I interrupted her. "Of course, that was very crass of me. Enjoy your evening, Lauren."

Tessa smiled with saccharin sweetness and waved her away with a flick of a wrist. "Goodbye Lauren. I'm sure you've got *things* to do."

The emphasis on the word made me glance at her curiously, but she simply shook her head. I could always get it out of her later.

After Lauren left and we finished dessert, I threw my napkin on the table. "Well, ladies, I'm off to bed. I have a big day tomorrow."

We said our goodbyes amid hugs and kisses and went our respective ways.

I walked out to my car not really paying much attention to my surroundings. I unlocked the door and got into the car, heading for home. Tessa had driven separately since she was meeting Jerome for a late night drink after his dinner meeting. I turned on my favorite tunes and thought about the evening with the girls. They always made me feel great. I was lucky to have them, and I knew it. Christina Aguilera's *Lady Marmalade* came on, and I began belting out the song, in support and comradery for women everywhere.

It was only at the end that I noticed the flashing lights behind me. Quickly pulling over, I reached for my purse, but it wasn't in the seat. A tap on my window had me quickly powering it down. "Hello, Officer. Was I doing something wrong?"

"I'd like to see your driver's license and registration please."

"Of course. May I reach into the glove compartment?"

"Yes."

He didn't seem to be the kind of man who talked pleasantries, so I reached into the glove compartment for the registration.

"Driver's license?"

"Well, you see it seems that I have inadvertently left my purse at the restaurant."

"Were you drinking, Ma'am?"

"I had one martini, but that was at least two hours ago. I had coffee, too." This was not going well. He was looking at me strangely.

"Please exit the vehicle, ma'am."

"Of course." This was getting worse by the minute.

"Can you please tell me your name?"

"Yes, Miranda Blake."

"Ma'am, do you realize you are operating a stolen vehicle?"

"What?" I screeched. "Absolutely not! This is my car." I pointed to my Volvo.

"Ma'am it's been reported as stolen by a Mister Daniel Blake."

"That's my ex-husband."

"Well, ma'am, it's registered to him." He tapped on the registration form. "And seeing as you have no identification,

I'm going to need to take you in until this matter can be settled."

"There's been a mistake! If you'll call him... here, you can have my phone, my cell phone–oh God it's in my purse! I can't go to jail! I can't believe this!" I babbled.

Suddenly, I was flipped over onto my stomach, lying across the hood of my car, my hands handcuffed behind my back. "Is this really necessary?" I growled.

He helped me upright, and his partner opened the back of the police cruiser. "Yes, ma'am. Standard procedure." His hand pressed down on my head, and I was gently maneuvered into the car.

Just when I thought my life was turning around, I was on my way to jail thanks to Rat Bastard.

Chapter Nine

After I had been "processed"–fingerprinted, photographed, and made to feel like the number they had me hold during said processing, I was led into a holding cell already occupied by three other women. "I'm innocent! I don't even have a parking ticket!"

Snorts and guffaws were heard after that remark. I cast the other inhabitants a disgusted glare and sat on the smelly cot. Apparently, the largest of the three took offense as she pushed herself off the wall and sat down next to me. I'd admit, I stiffened in fear when she put her rather beefy hand on my knee. "First time, sugar? Don't worry 'bout it none. I'll have my man, Donetter, vouch for you. You treat him right, and you'll be back on the streets in no time."

In shock, I took a detailed observation of my cellmates.

One was young, barely eighteen–if that. She had that defiant 'fuck you' air about her, but she was painfully thin. Torn fishnet stockings, six-inch heels with spikes, and more black on her eyes than a coal miner. Her hair was black as well, which made her white face and blood red lips even more prominent. The other was older, maybe thirty, with blonde frizzy hair decorated a giant plaid bow. The corset barely contained her enormous breasts, and her skirt was simply a short band of latex. Her thigh high boots had an image of snarling dragons on them.

Donetter's woman appeared to be the oldest and the largest at almost six feet tall. She wore a gold sequined mini dress, gladiator sandals, and her makeup was almost cartoonish it was so bright. She also had an Adam's apple.

I scooted out from under her hand. "Thank you, um…"

"Diana."

"Yes, Diana, but I don't think that will be necessary. As soon as I get my phone call, I'll be out of here."

"Uh huh." The others snickered.

I hastened to explain, "No really! This is all a mistake. My rat bastard ex-husband said I stole a car, but it's *my* car." My shoulders slumped slightly. "It may be in his name, but everything is. That's why this divorce has been so difficult."

I noticed the other two coming closer. "You got a rat bastard ex-husband?" Snarling Dragon Boots asked.

I nodded. "He took everything because it was in his name, but he didn't bother with the car. I wonder why…" I shook my head. "No matter. After twenty-five years, I'm finally free, and I'm going to live a guilt-free life."

"After you get out of jail," the youngest one sniggered.

"Shut up, Jacinda. You ain't getting out no time soon either."

Diana shushed the two of them. "You or he get the divorce?"

"Him, but I'm glad. Like I said, I'm free and tired of being a doormat." I stood up and began pacing the cell. "What I don't understand is why tonight? We don't keep in contact. He didn't know I'd be out," I stopped suddenly. "Of course! Lauren must have called him!" I nodded at their perplexed expression.

"Who the fuck is Laura?" the youngest one asked.

"Lauren. She's my boss' girlfriend or hostess or whatever." I waved my hands. "It doesn't matter. Apparently, she wasn't too happy to hear us talking about Reed."

"Who?" Diane demanded.

"Reed Michaels is my boss. I was out with my friends and she was in the same restaurant. But why would she do that?"

Diana shrugged. "Prolly cause your boss wants to fuck you."

"What?!" I gasped loudly. "Uh, no. That's not true. Most of the time, I think he can barely tolerate me."

Dragon Boots touched my hair. It was a bit disconcerting. "You're attractive for an old lady. Got that kinda body men want—not too skinny, not too fat. Something to hold onto when they get to rockin'."

My face went up in flames as a picture of Reed doing the dirty came to mind.

"Uh oh! Girl, you want him too!" Diane exclaimed. She

stood up and twerked, slapping the air. The others followed her, dancing around the room, making sexual moans and sounds. I laughed.

The booking officer, Burroughs, peeked in and snarled, "Quiet!"

I immediately sat down and shut up, then popped up in anger. "I know my rights! I watched Law and Order. Where's my phone call?" I shouted. My cellmates started chanting "phone call" and banged on the bars.

Burroughs wasn't impressed. "You'll get your phone call when I'm good and damn ready and not before. Keep it up and I'll detain all of you over the weekend." He closed the main door once again.

I sat down, dejected.

What seemed like an eternity, but was probably less than an hour later, the door opened, and Officer Burroughs unlocked my cell. "One call. You give me trouble, and I'll put you back in cuffs."

I shook my head vehemently in understanding. I definitely didn't wish to be back in those wrist biters.

"What about us?" Diane shouted.

"You've had your call. Guess Donetter ain't got the scratch."

He led me to the outer office hall, where the pay phone was located. I would have to call collect as they had taken everything when they booked me. I'd had a bit to think about it, and decided the best course of action was Tessa, because wherever Tessa was, Jerome, her lawyer husband, was bound to be nearby.

I heard Tessa answer, and I shouted her name as the

operator asked for acceptance. Almost immediately–thank-fully–her beautiful voice came across the line, every syllable full of worry. "Miranda! What's happened?"

"Rat Bastard had me arrested for stealing my own car! Help!" I began to cry. It was all too much.

"Miranda! Stop! We're on our way."

I sniffled a goodbye and reluctantly returned the phone to Officer Burroughs. He gave me a nod. "Cheer up. You got help on the way. It's more than I can say about your friends in there." He motioned to the cell room.

I returned to the cell and let the ladies know I had contacted Tessa. Diana asked how I knew her, and I began to tell stories of how I met each of my friends. I ended with Kimy shooting my jet tub. They laughed, and Dragon Boots, whose real name was Tawanda, asked me about my lip color, which led to a discussion about what makeup was good to use, and then the young one, Bailey, started a conversation about fashion trends.

I was telling them about my lack of grace in the high heel department and how Reed had bought me tennis shoes for the office when the outer door opened and in stepped the man himself accompanied by officer Burroughs. I wondered if it was too late to try and flush myself down that incredibly disgusting toilet in the corner.

"Holy Fuck!" Towanda exclaimed.

"I call dibs!" Bailey sauntered over to the bars.

Diane stood in front of me. "This that Rat Bastard, Sugar?" She looked pissed.

I hastened to correct her, "Oh no! This is my boss, Reed

Michaels." I scooted past her. "Reed, I'd like you to meet Diana, Tawanda, and Bailey."

In true Reed fashion, he didn't blink an eye. "Ladies, it's lovely meeting you. Thank you for taking such good care of my…of Miranda."

My three new friends, streetwise and experienced, could still blush on occasion. They nodded but kept silent.

I understood the feeling all too well. Reed Michaels was in full confidence mode, and he was a sight to behold in his Tom Ford suit. He reeked of money, power, and, well, Reed. Especially when he was focusing his eyes on you such as he was doing to me. He was smooth and charming, but I saw the anger behind his eyes. Suddenly, I wasn't sure I wanted to go with him.

"Miranda? Shall we?"

Officer Burroughs hastened to unlock the cell door, and I stepped out on shaky limbs. He started to close it, but Reed spoke up. "Ladies? Are you coming?"

When Burroughs started to protest, Reed simply quirked a supercilious eyebrow. My new friends didn't need to be asked twice and were simpering all over him. Tawanda and Bailey latched onto his elbows like leeches, leaving Diana and me to follow out into the main area. In less time than it takes to catch a cab in Chicago, we were free, and the ladies hugged me. We exchanged cell numbers, and they went on their merry way.

I, on the other hand, was immediately enclosed within the confines of the back seat of a top of the line Mercedes, sitting next to an extremely annoyed Reed.

"Home, James."

I moved to correct him, but Reed shot me such a look of such fury, daring me to say anything, I acquiesced. Apparently, I was going home with Reed.

Chapter Ten

The silence in the car was deafening. I couldn't stand it. *When had I ever been able to stay quiet?* "Reed, I'm sorry —" I began to apologize, but he held up a hand, his anger coming off of him in waves. I scooted into the corner, near the door, and lowered my head.

Now that the evening was over, the relief of it all brought tears to my eyes. I brushed them away with my hand, but my nerves weren't through with me yet. I started to shake with the aftermath. It was my typical response to a crisis—stand up, get done what needs to be done, then break-down after. From my child's broken arm to the death of my parents, this was my M.O.

The inner privacy window raised. Seconds later, Reed pulled me into his arms, my legs across his lap.

He didn't tell me not to cry, he simply offered me his

handkerchief. Such a gentlemanly thing—a small mono-grammed kerchief—very Reed-like.

"I'm sorry," I blubbered against his chest. "I don't know why now—"

"It's a normal response to the adrenalin rush of danger," He stated calmly. "Everyone has it to some degree, even me."

"You cry?"

He continued to stroke my arm in comfort. "No, I have sex."

I jerked up at that, hitting him in the chin with my head.

"Ouch!" he yelled.

"Sorry!" I tried to scramble off him, but he held fast.

"I was joking, Miranda...well, mostly." He laid my head back down on him. "Trying for levity. My apologies."

"I guess you do have that adrenaline high when you do business acquisitions. What do you really do?" I tried to snuggle in a bit closer without him noticing. Reed smelled so nice. His fingers caressing my skin...it was lovely to be held and comforted. *Don't go there, Miranda. He's your boss.*

"I don't get high off business dealings or afraid either. I know what I'm doing."

I peered up at him. He still appeared pissed. "Then how do you know about the aftermath from danger"?"

"Ritter."

"He told you?"

"No, I've been getting him out of serious trouble since we were teens."

I digested that for a moment. Tessa and Chloe had said

something similar. "The kind where you were in danger, too?"

"Sometimes."

I scrambled up. The talk about Ritter had me thinking of my earrings. I grabbed the bag I was given with my personal effects and pulled them out.

"Don't." Reed laid his hand on mine. "I'd like one night without the reminder of Ritter."

I conceded. I wasn't sure what to say about that. But there was something I did need to know. "Are you still angry with me?" I murmured.

He didn't meet my eyes. "I was never angry at you. At the situation, your ex-husband, and Ritter, yes, but not at you."

"Ritter? I don't understand."

Reed sighed, laying his head back on the rest and closing his eyes. "I'm sorry, Miranda, but Ritter was with me when you called Tessa. His response was typical Ritter. He said it was a shame, hoped I wouldn't fire you, then took off for his night of fun."

I shrugged. "OK, it's a bit callous, but I called Tessa, not him."

Reed jackknifed back into position, pulling me up to look at him, his were eyes blazing. "When are you going to understand, woman?! You are beautiful, talented, and sexy, but Ritter will never truly have a relationship with anyone. You are pining for someone who only cares about himself, and that will never change. Not even your love can do that."

I pushed away from him. "My *love?* What in the world are you talking about? Ritter and I are JUST FRIENDS.

Why doesn't anyone believe that?" I threw my hands up in the air. "We've never even slept together. Hell, he only kissed me once."

The intercom buzzed. Without taking his eyes from mine, Reed pushed the button, "Yes?"

"Sir, we've arrived."

"Thank you, James."

Seconds later, James opened the door. I said hello to him, asked after his welfare, and tried to think of something else to say to avoid going up those steps and into Reed's house.

It didn't work, and I found myself entering Reed's magnificent home. He ushered me into what appeared to be a library. Taking a seat on the sofa near the fireplace, the warmth from the fire gave me a sense of comfort and safety. Or maybe it was the man standing before me.

"Ritter said he was in a relationship with you."

"Why would he say that? It's not true." I wasn't sure if I should stay seated or not. This appeared to be a serious conversation if the expression on his face was any indication. I'd never seen him appear this intense. Reed took my indecision away by placing both hands on the arms of the chair and leaning in.

"It's not?" he murmured as he searched my eyes.

"No! How many times do I—" My thoughts and words were abruptly cut-off as Reed pushed his lips to mine. Soft, gentle, swift. I didn't have time to react.

He pulled back, searching my face again. Satisfied with what he saw there, he kissed me again, this time with more force, his hands coming up to cup my face. I opened for him, felt his tongue enter, tempting mine. He tasted of whiskey and mint. I knew I wasn't fresh and sweet. The thought had me pulling away.

"No," he groaned against my lips. He lifted me up from the chair and took my place, settling me on his lap, never breaking the kiss.

When he lifted his lips, I sucked in a heavy breath and ventured a peek at him. He, too, was breathing rapidly, but the fire of desire burned in his eyes with such intensity it almost frightened me. "I want you, Miranda. So much." He glanced down at my body sprawled across his lap. "So damn much."

This was wrong, all kinds of wrong, but it didn't seem to matter. I could smell my own arousal, feel my damp panties, and I was sitting on his very hard erection. I peered into his eyes. His control was there, as always, beneath that incredible layer of desire. If I wished him to stop, he would, and there would be no other chance.

But I didn't want him to stop. Even more than that, I wanted to give him everything, to shatter that damn control, to show him I wanted *him*, not the chairman of the board, or the heir to a fortune. No, I wanted the *man*. The man who still carried handkerchiefs, who took the time to help a friend, the man who did so much for everyone else. God, his honor and noble nature was such a turn on to me.

"Yes, Reed. I want you, too." I kissed his neck.

His growl confirmed my acceptance as he began to unzip my dress, kissing the exposed flesh. Too much flesh in my mind. I tried to hide my poochy parts, but he stopped my hands. "You are beautiful, Miranda. A Botticelli model of perfection." His hand skimmed across my stomach. He kissed between my breasts. "So womanly, so soft. Let me show you." He kissed me again with such hunger I had to believe him.

When I wiggled against him, lifting up to help him relieve me of my panties, he groaned, "I want to see you spread out before me, the firelight flickering against your skin." He plucked at my nipple.

He could have me any way he desired. I hungered for him. I tried to gracefully rise from his lap to lay down on the rug, but somehow, my feet got tangled with his, and I sort of rolled down his legs and flopped onto my ass near his feet, my legs spread wide apart and my elbows supporting my upper body, fully exposed and not feeling nearly as sexy as I had a minute ago.

Reed didn't say a word. He simply stared at me with his dark eyes. I could feel my blush heating my face. He came down on one knee, still fully clothed. I watched as he ran one finger lightly down my torso to the top of my mound. My pulse quickened at the touch. "So sensitive," he murmured. His finger skimmed back up, this time circling the outside of my breasts. My nipples hardened, and my breasts grew heavy. He blew lightly across my skin. *What was he doing?*

I made to shift my legs as the cool air was doing erotic things to my body. I was warmed from the fire, cooled by his breath, and fully exposed to his gaze. I thought I would feel embarrassed or awkward, this first time with another man, but, no. Reed took away the fear simply by gazing at me with such blatant desire. I had no doubt that he was pleased with what he discovered beneath my clothes.

Reed touched my foot, stilling my movement. He slid his gentle finger along the bottom of my foot, making me giggle at the caress. "Ah, the beauty is also ticklish." He repeated the stroke on my other foot. "Mm, this brings up a wealth of possibilities."

His stare zeroed in on the apex of my legs. I tightened and arched. I couldn't help it. I desperately wanted him to touch me there. I was practically wanton with desire, and he'd barely laid a hand on me.

He stood up suddenly and reached out a hand. "Stand up, love."

What? Confused, I did as he asked, bewildered by his order. *Weren't we going to…? Had he changed his mind?* I crossed my arms in front of me.

"No!" He exclaimed. "Come back to me, my beauty." He pulled my arms away, forcing me to drop them. "I want to watch you undress me, to feel your hands on me." His lips found mine again, tender and sweet.

I melted once again.

When he ended the kiss, I slid my hands into his suit jacket, sliding it off his shoulders, dropping it onto a nearby chair. I realized at that moment a full-length mirror hung near the door. He could feel my hands on him and watch me in the mirror. Rather than being shy, it emboldened me. focused his buttons, kissing the skin as it became exposed until I ended on my haunches, his erection close to my lips. I rubbed my nose against the cloth. He gasped.

As the last of the buttons gave way, I pulled his shirt

from his waistband, sliding up the length of his body, making sure my breasts touched his chest on the way up. I wished I could play, prove I was up to the task of being a sexy lover, but my own juices were trickling down my thigh.

And Reed had had enough foreplay.

He pulled my hair, forcing my mouth up for his kiss, and he took possession of my body and my will. We came up for air, and he immediately pushed me down to my knees.

I eagerly went to work on his belt and pants, freeing his erection, running a finger over the top to capture that drip of arousal. Watching him in the mirror as he stared at me, I put it slowly to my mouth, licking my finger, sucking it, never breaking eye contact.

His growl was my undoing. I fell sideways onto the rug as he came down over me. Kissing me with such pent up passion, I couldn't think straight. Soon, he moved lower, raining nibbles on my breasts as his fingers slid down my stomach and into me. His thumb pressed against the top of my mound, rubbing my clit as his fingers pressed up and up...I suddenly came with a scream; however, Reed wasn't finished yet. Before I could catch my breath, he was there, lapping at my folds, his tongue doing magical, naughty things which had me soaring again.

I loved it but craved him, feeling him, all of him. So far, I had been the only one overwhelmed with pleasure. *Was I doing something wrong?* I glanced down. *No, fully hard and heavy.* I tried to wrap my hand around him, but he sucked my nipple into his mouth as his hands pulled mine above my head, holding them there. Obviously, he didn't want my hands on his body. *What was going on?* Just a minute ago, he was letting me touch him.

"Miranda!"

I jerked back to reality, noting my errant thoughts had had an effect on my libido. My juicy parts weren't doing their part. I scooted out from under him.

Reed lithely stretched out beside me. "Where did you go? Did I do something unpleasant?"

I noticed he was now semi-erect and laid stiffly next to me. How do I explain? "No! It was wonderful."

He grimaced.

"No! It was more than I…um…so much more…" I trailed off.

He laid his arm over his eyes. "Then what? You shut down. If we are going to be lovers, I need to know."

I lifted onto my side. "Are we lovers, Reed?"

"I don't do this with just anyone, Miranda, therefore, the answer is yes." He catapulted up. "Is this about your job?"

"My job? No, not my job," I said.

He was completely flaccid now and didn't appear very lover-like either. Frustrated and annoyed, he needed an honest answer and deserved it. "It's about my performance," I whispered.

"Your performance? I don't understand. You were faking it?" He looked appalled, and I hastened to reassure him. "

"Oh no! No! You made me… multiple times, and I was…couldn't you tell?" Now, I was frustrated.

"Then what performance, Miranda?"

God this was extremely embarrassing! "I've only had

one lover, my ex-husband. I must not be doing something right, or you'd be in me by now." I rattled off in a rush, hiding my face in my knees.

Reed sighed, pulling on my arm until I settled in next to him again. I still couldn't meet his gaze. "I'm sorry, love. I'm sorry you've had such a mediocre experience. Look at me, Miranda."

After slowly lifting my head, he kissed me tenderly. Pulling back, he told me, "The reason I didn't want you to touch me was that I knew if you did, it would completely unman me. I desire to be inside you when that happens."

I shook my head. "Then why?"

He chuckled. "Oh, Miranda, love, I wished to prolong the moment...our time together," he kissed me again. "I wanted to pleasure you again and again until you lost control."

"I did!"

"No, love. You held back. I could feel it. I don't just want your orgasms, I want all of your desires—no holding back."

I began to laugh. "Oh, Reed, I held back because you were holding back."

He flipped me over, hovering above me. "Then give it to me, love. And I'll do the same."

He settled fully upon me, nuzzling my breasts, nipping, plucking, then reaching down to test my readiness. I, for my part, squeezed and rubbed him until he was hard.

He positioned himself, his cock rubbing against my entrance, and he smiled. "We are being awfully cliché doing this by the fire."

"That's OK," I gasped as he entered me, and I stretched

around his girth. He was much larger than rat bastard–I couldn't help except compare. "Next, we'll do it in the butler's pantry."

He chuckled as he pumped into me faster and harder. "Every fucking room of this mansion."

I grabbed his fine ass, digging my nails into his flesh, and lifted my hips. "Damn straight."

It took us all weekend, but we kept that promise.

Chapter Eleven

I t wasn't long before Agnes knew about my relationship with Reed. I managed to keep her in the dark for about three days. However, right before my lunch break on the third day, she marched over to my desk and barked, "Conference Room—now!" I immediately jumped up and followed her, wondering what I had done wrong. I didn't have to wait to find out.

"Why on earth did you not tell me you and Reed were seeing each other?" she demanded as she closed the door. "I've been acting like a fool, trying to tempt Reed to ask you out." She sat down in the nearest chair with a huff, crossing her arms over her chest. "I even offered to house sit that damn dog of yours."

She was hurt. I could see it in her eyes. Sitting in the chair beside her, I squeezed her hand. "I'm sorry, Agnes. It's not that I didn't want to tell you, but it's early yet, and if it doesn't work out, I didn't want you…" I trailed off. The fact was I wasn't sure whose side she would take, and the last thing I wished to do was put her in that kind of position.

"You didn't know which way I'd land. I understand, Miranda. I don't think you should be thinking of what-ifs right now, dear. It's more than apparent he's smitten."

I grinned at her use of those old-fashioned words. "How do you know he's smitten?" I teased.

"He hasn't fired anyone in two days!" Agnes guffawed.

I laughed. "Reed doesn't fire people. He relocates them. But, to confirm, yes, Reed and I are seeing each other. It's new, and I'd rather not make him feel awkward at work, ergo, I'm not telling anyone."

Agnes shook her head. "People will find out. You can't keep this kind of thing a secret too long, but I, for one, am pleased as punch. Two of my favorite people together at last," she cackled in glee. "I can't wait to plan the wedding."

"Agnes! Stop! We haven't even been out to dinner yet."

"That's true. We ordered in." Reed said from the doorway.

I screamed and almost fell out of the chair thanks to the rollers on the bottom. Reed prevented my accident by putting a foot on the chair leg.

"Good God, Reed! How many times did she fall out of bed?" Agnes grabbed my arm to help me back into the chair to sit properly.

"She didn't. I had a hand on her the whole time." Reed winked at me.

"I bet you did, you rascal." Agnes stood. "Well, I'm off

to actually get some work done. Oh, and, Miranda, if you need to get rid of those earrings from Ritter…" She pointed to her ears. "See you kids later." With a wave and a whiff of Bengay, she was gone.

Funny, I hadn't thought about those earrings since the night Reed bailed me out of jail. They sat, forgotten, in my ring holder on my vanity. Maybe I should give them to Agnes.

I came back to the moment as Reed leaned over the chair back and pulled my hair to the side, kissing my neck. "Um, the conference room is all glass, Reed. Are you sure you should be doing this?" Oh heavens, my panties were already damp!

"Making it easier for you not to be conflicted about our relationship," he murmured as he tugged my ear between his lips. I tilted to give him better access to my neck. "Mm, there's that tasty spot." His breath teased against my skin, making me shiver in desire. I knew that naughty tongue was about to…ah, God, I loved it when he licked the spot at the curve of my neck.

"You want me to tell people?" I moaned as he nipped gently.

"I don't give a damn who knows, Miranda. You're mine." He straightened up, noticed the crowd gathered near the windows.

He helped me out of my chair, holding my hand and opened the conference room door. "We are going to lunch, ladies and gentlemen. And if I'm lucky, it will be a long lunch."

The crowd cheered, and I blushed crimson, but I truly did hope it would be a long lunch as well.

THREE WEEKS INTO OUR RELATIONSHIP, it dawned on me he never spent the night at my place. I wanted him there, to gather some memories of us as a couple in my space, too. Besides, I wanted to cook for him. Totally old fashioned, 1950's housewife syndrome, or whatever you chose to call it. I wanted to prepare a divine dinner for my man, and I decided to do just that.

I informed Agnes of my plan, and she contacted James and told him to pack a bag for the boss. He was spending the night with his gal.

I also told Tessa and the girls. They had taken to "dropping in" whenever, and I didn't think Reed would appreciate that.

"Make sure you're prepared, honey. I've got some champagne and strawberries up at the house, and they are yours. I'll stock it before we leave for our trip. I'll miss you while I'm gone, but I won't worry now that I know Reed will be there," Tessa gushed over the phone.

Next came Sadie. "Do you need an aphrodisiac or a cleansing of the bedroom to erase old lovers?" she asked. "I've got a new supply of sage." I politely declined, reminding her that no other lover had ever been present.

Kimy and Chloe simply wished me luck and reminded me to keep condoms in the nightstand drawer. I doubted I needed to worry about an STD with this particular

Michaels brother, but I assured them I would. No need to share we'd been doing it bareback for almost a month.

I left early Friday to prepare for Reed. He loved Italian food, so that was what I chose to cook. I made a simple antipasto for starters, then my spaghetti carbonara, and finished with coffee and a pineapple whipped dessert. With my food preparations complete, I took my time in the ritual of prepping for my man. I was daydreaming about Reed when I heard Prince bark. "Quiet, Prince. You're killing my mojo!"

The bathroom door opened, and Reed stepped in, toeing off his shoes. "We wouldn't want that, now would we, love?"

I was still gaping as he divested himself of the rest of his clothes and stepped into my bubble bath. "I'll kiss you as soon as you get rid of that green stuff on your face."

Oh Lordy! I hastily scrubbed my face clean of the facial mask. "Much better." I heard Reed mutter before he took my breath away with his dominating kisses.

"Anything we need to worry about in the kitchen?" he asked after a bit. He was mounding bubbles upon my breasts as he sat behind me.

"No," I panted out. His nimble fingers plucked at my nipples as he nibbled at my neck.

"Mm, Good. I want you now," he stated, spinning me around and settling me on his hard cock. I slid effortlessly onto him, as my body took over, gyrating, bouncing, loving how quickly he could make me a quivering mess of climax.

"That's it. God, you are so open in your loving." He reached between us, pinching my clit, and I went wild, pulling his hair, sloshing water, squeezing him within me. I'd never felt anything like this. I fell against him when I came back to earth, and he wrapped his arms around me, hugging me tightly.

We eventually dried off and dressed. Dinner was ready, and Prince was, for once, quiet and calm. Reed enjoyed the pasta and the conversation, but the moments of silence were filled with sensual glances. I cleared the table and offered him coffee and dessert. "I want my dessert in bed, love," he declared.

Reed's desire was so damn intense. His words, his touch, everything focused on me alone. I whipped around, throwing my arms around his neck. "As you wish, love."

He kissed me long and hard before leading me to bed and gave his all to give me pleasure. I was possessed, body and soul, by Reed Michaels. And when I was finally allowed to rest, I knew what Kimy meant about a "fantasm". It was the most fantastic orgasm a woman can have because she gives herself over to her lover: mind, body, and soul. It was time to face the fact I was completely in love with Reed Michaels.

TWO NIGHTS LATER, we were in bed, finally eating that pineapple whip when Reed asked me if Ritter had ever asked me to spy on him. I was nonplussed and shook my head. "Absolutely not! He knew I would never do something like that." I put down my dessert and faced him. "Why would you ask?"

He shrugged. "You know the takeover attempt was thwarted, but there's something brewing with the board. I can't put my finger on it, but I've got a feeling Ritter's involved." He cleaned the last of the pineapple with his spoon. "This was good." He reached over and kissed me. "But not as tasty as you."

How on earth did he always know the right thing to say to make me shiver with need?

"I want you again." He slid the sheet down, exposing my breasts.

"Reed, tell me about this hunch you have. I'd like to help."

The sheet slid down further and Reed did, too. "After." He spread my legs.

"After what?" I teased him, grinning.

He peeked up from between my legs. "After another dessert. I'm still hungry."

I sighed and opened for him. I *had* promised to feed him.

After another round of "dessert", I got back to his comments about the company and Ritter. When he realized I wasn't going to let it go, he sat up against the headboard, pulling me up to rest against his chest.

"When I was eight years old, I learned I had a brother. A half-brother, Ritter. Apparently, my father had had an affair, well, he had many, but the only one that produced a child, as far as I know, was this one. The woman interrupted my birthday party to bring Ritter to my father, dumped him actually in the driveway near the gate and left."

"Oh, how terrible!"

"Well, I didn't think so. I thought he was the very best

birthday present ever. And he was my best friend for a while. Anyway, it was in high school when I found out how my life was truly going to be. I was groomed and tested, sent to the very best private prep schools, while Ritter, who I believed to be as smart as me in other ways, was sent to the military school. Father had an heir, he didn't need a spare, especially one that reminded him of his transgressions."

He cleared his throat and continued, "I came back from school, eager to tell Ritter all about it, only to find he had been expelled. Apparently, he couldn't keep it in his pants any better than my father could, but that didn't matter to my parents. He was out of the will, out of the house, and out of our lives."

I looked up at him. "But you didn't allow that, did you?"

"No. I couldn't. It was actually the first fight I ever had with my parents. I found Ritter and set him up in his own place. I realized he couldn't work at Michaels Group as long as Father ran things, so I found him a job with a friend's father."

"It means he got some business acumen after all!" I said. "Very smart, Reed!"

"Well, actually, he seduced my friend's sister. He then ran off to Barbados when angry Daddy came to me for vindication because his daughter had been discarded. That was the first of many buy offs for dear Ritter."

"Well, you are much more forgiving than I would have been. The ingrate!"

Reed chuckled at my indignation. "It was the path of least resistance, believe me. Forgiveness had nothing to do with it. I was learning the business and didn't have time to deal with his shenanigans. It was only after Father died and I inherited everything, that Ritter came back into my life."

I kissed his chin. "And you took him back like the prodigal son."

"Not quite. You see, I owed him in a way. Finding him in bed with my then fiancée opened my eyes to both his ways and hers. I figured the best place for him was near me since it makes keeping tabs on him a little easier."

"You still held out hope that he would turn his life around? Oh, Reed, after what he did?"

"Nope. I knew that it would be impossible. Until you." He trailed his finger across my cheek. "You had redemption for the hopeless written all over you."

"Me?"

"Yes, I saw you across the room at the restaurant with my brother, and for the first time in my life, I desired what he had. It wasn't a comfortable feeling, and I realized this was what Ritter had experienced all those years."

I sighed. "Ritter and I could never be anything more than friends, Reed. He didn't make my heart flip like you do." I kissed him passionately before settling back against his chest once again.

"I'm not sure we are going to be able to be anything anymore, love. His bid to take over the company isn't simply a flight of fancy. He's swayed a few on the board. I just wish I understood why. I haven't curtailed his outings. His income stream is solid."

"Maybe it's his big play to be the man his father never gave him credit for."

"Well, I'm not my father, but I won't allow him to take

the company my family has worked so hard to maintain and expand. Thousands of people would be let go. He can't keep it going. With him at the helm, he will dismantle and sell it to our competition. No, this will be the end of our relationship if he succeeds."

Running a hand through his hair, he sighed. "I'm going to call a meeting of my friends on the board and let them know Ritter's plan. Maybe they can sway the others back to me. As it is, it will be a close call, but I'm still in charge. I'm only glad Ritter doesn't know about the hit we took on the new software app the R &D department has in progress. Some of the research was stolen, but we caught the guy. What he did manage to take may place us second in the running with the new technology, but only if he found the right buyer and they use it before we can get it into production."

"What can I do to help, Reed?"

"Feed me for starters. I'm starving."

I giggled and wrapped the sheet around my body to head to the kitchen.

I washed my hands. "So you're hungry are you?"

He grabbed my sheet, tugging me to him. "For you? Always."

"For food," I snickered.

"Can you cook naked?" He nibbled on my neck.

I felt the now familiar tingle of desire, but my tummy rumbled. "Anything except bacon, baby." I sighed happily, stretching my neck to allow better access.

"Got an apron?" He kissed me, licking my lips.

"Want to play naughty housewife, do you?"

"Mm, how about strawberries and whipped cream?" He pinched my nipple.

"Funny you should ask…" I opened the fridge and took out Tessa's gift. Reed grabbed the champagne, and we headed back to the bed.

Chapter Twelve

I arrived Monday morning with the required Starbucks and donuts that had become a ritual for me and the security guy. George saw me at the door and hurried to open it, grabbing his coffee and the donut bag.

"Thanks, it's really brisk out there today. Should have rethought the footwear." I glanced down at my black kitten heels. They weren't above two inches, with a tiny stem to stand on. And they looked fabulous with my new red power suit.

"Typical Chicago weather ain't nothing compared to the storm brewing up top."

"What storm?" I took a sip of my warm brew and headed for the elevator. He followed beside me.

"Word is that there was a big meeting Sunday night right here. The board of Directors and the boss. Seems little man Ritter tried to worm his way in where he doesn't belong."

Hmm, I had left Reed's bed Sunday morning. We had texted throughout the day, but he never mentioned a meeting. The big showdown might have been a surprise. Ritter would want every advantage.

"Thanks for the heads up, George. I'll see you later." I entered the elevator and headed to the top floor wondering what was in store for me today.

Agnes greeted me as soon as the doors opened. "Thank God! He's in a foul mood. He wants you in his office immediately." I handed her my coffee and hurried ahead. Whatever his mood, I had to find out exactly what happened.

I took a breath as I neared the closed door to his office, smoothing my hair and plastering a smile on my face. I stepped up and knocked.

"Come in."

I couldn't help the shiver up my spine. Reed's voice was cold as ice. I opened the door. His back was to me, staring out the massive bank of windows.

"Reed," I rushed into the room, "I just heard about the meeting. What happened?"

He spun around as I walked closer to his desk. The sunlight framed his form but left his face in shadow. "I thought you would know, Miranda." His voice was soft but lethal.

"Me?" I approached him, reaching out to touch him. I pulled back as his fierce visage came sharply into focus.

"Yes, you, my lying little bitch. Ritter called the meeting last night to tell them about the research theft."

I shrank back. "What?" My mind went blank.

Reed advanced, grabbing my arms, giving me a shake. "How could you? What do you have to gain, Miranda? Did Ritter promise you a percentage of the sale? A position on another board? His undying affection? Why the fuck did you do it?"

"I... I didn't! I didn't tell him!" My mind whirled. How did Ritter find out?

Reed suddenly let me go, and I stumbled, falling to the floor. He made no effort to help me up, glaring down at me in disgust. I couldn't hold his gaze. It hurt too much. My heart was breaking.

Reed marched away from me. "Well, it didn't work. I got the news that our production is ready to be unveiled. We won't do it up big, but simply get it out there to as many companies as possible as fast as we can."

He sat down in his immense leather chair, watching me as I gathered myself, getting up on shaking knees. "Reed, please. You can't believe I would ever say anything to Ritter. I would never betray you." Tears fell, my nose was running, but I didn't care. I had to make him believe me.

"Save it, Miranda." He held up his hand. "I want you and your shit out of my office and out of my life immediately. Security will see you out."

I stood stock still. This man...this wasn't my Reed. My lover, the protective gentleman of my dreams. No, this was the ruthless man his father had created, but I'd be damned if I was going to be thrown out like a piece of trash. I gathered my dignity like a cloak around me. "I will find out how

Ritter knew about the theft. And when I do, I'll make sure you understand I had nothing to do with it."

He waved his hand in dismissal, not even looking at me. "Don't bother. Ritter is gone for good, and the board is firmly on my side. Goodbye, Miranda."

He never glanced up as I shuffled across the room where the security guard and Agnes waited by the door.

I gathered my things from my desk.

"Miranda", Agnes said softly, "He didn't mean it. He's furious, but when he calms down, he will realize you couldn't have had anything to do with this. It's not in your nature."

I couldn't meet her gaze. I would start crying again, *feeling* again if I did. Right now, a pleasant numbness invaded my soul. "It doesn't matter. He believed someone else. He didn't ask or hesitate. He believed."

"Honey, are you sure Ritter didn't overhear you talking to one of your friends about it?"

I shook my head. "I would never tell his secrets. Not to anyone. He should understand that."

"He will come to his senses and—" Agnes began, but I interrupted her.

"You can have those earrings from Ritter. I'll send them to you."

"I don't want anything from that man! But I want you to be the bigger person here, Miranda."

I could finally look at her, furious that once again I had to cater to a man. "Well, I'm tired of being the bigger person. I've been the doormat for one man and now a whipping post for another. I'm done." I gave her a hug and then picked up my meager possessions. "Keep in touch, dear. I'll miss you." To my ears, I sounded cold and dismissive, but I couldn't allow more. I held a fragile thread on my emotions as it was.

Nodding to the security guard, I headed for the elevator, somewhat ready to meet whatever life was going to throw my way next. I heard Agnes yell to wait, but I allowed the doors to shut. I only wish I could shut off my heartbreak as easily.

I nodded to George who hastened to open the doors to allow me to exit. "You didn't do it, Miz Blake. He'll come crawling back begging forgiveness."

"Thank you, George." I couldn't look at him. Only a few more steps and I would be free from the Michaels brothers forever. I moved into the sunny, cold morning.

Holding the bag with my stuff in one hand, I searched for the keys to my car in my purse, the car Reed had arranged to have returned to me. Just as I reached them, my elbow was tugged. Jerking my head up, I met the serious gaze of Ritter. Fury once again flowed through me.

"I know it looks bad, Miranda, but if you will come with me, you'll understand." He grabbed me by the arm and steered me to his Mercedes parked near the curb.

I tried to wrestle away from him. "I'm not going anywhere with you!" I got loose and spun away from him, moving quickly.

Arms wrapped around me from behind, and I was lifted off my feet, making me drop my bag in the process. "Let me go! Ritter, dammit!"

He ignored me, heading back to his car. The passenger door was open, and he tried to shove me inside.

I kicked the door shut. "Let me go or I'll scream!"

"Stop it, Miranda. I need you!" He opened the door once again. I kicked it shut again.

"Goddammit!" Ritter shouted. "You are coming with me!"

I bit his arm, hard. He dropped me, and I landed on my butt. I started to crawl away, but a gun in my face stopped me. "I'm sorry, Miranda. But I need Reed to see reason, and the only way that's going to happen is for me to have some leverage." He helped me to my feet. I slapped his hand when it tried to grab me again and brushed my hair away from my face.

"Well, you picked the wrong leverage. You would have done better with Agnes. Reed is done with me thanks to you. He thinks I told you about the research theft."

Ritter pushed the gun into my back. "You did, indirectly. Get walking."

I hesitated. If I stepped into the car, I didn't know what would happen, but the fact that he was willing to point a gun at me–I decided it wasn't going to be good. I began walking. "Tell me how you knew." *That's it, Miranda. Pander to his ego. Let him think he's in control until you can come up with a way out of this mess.* Who was I kidding? He had a gun! He was definitely in charge.

"It was the earrings. I knew when Lauren told me how frantic Reed was when you fell at the ball, he was enamored of you. Figured it wouldn't hurt to keep tabs on you while I worked the board to my way of thinking. I couldn't believe my luck when he took you to bed." He opened the car door. "When he told you about the research problem, I knew I had what I needed to win, but I had to act fast."

"Lauren? She was telling you Reed's secrets?"

"She was more than happy to share anything and every-thing after Reed refused to save her company."

He pushed the gun into my back. "Get in the car."

I had no choice. I shifted toward the passenger side.

"Miranda! Don't you dare!"

I glanced up to see Reed heading down the steps, looking like the Devil Incarnate. My knight in shining Armani had arrived.

Chapter Thirteen

"Stop, Reed! I'll shoot her!" Ritter shouted, waving his gun at Reed. Some of the gathering crowd screamed, others ran, and a few continued to stand in morbid fascination of the scene playing out before them. George stood next to my lover, every inch the powerful security guard he was hired to be.

I'd like to think it was my love for Reed that made me do it, perhaps my concern for his safety, or even the thought of life without him, but, no, it was the heel of my shoe that saved the love of my life. When Ritter pointed the gun at Reed, he jerked me forward. My sexy kitten heels came in contact with the sidewalk grate, finding the hole in the grid, and I stumbled, crashing into Ritter. He went down, the gun in his hand discharged as I fell on top of him. I was afraid to move. I didn't think I'd been shot, but if I moved, I might realize I had been.

Ritter screamed in agony, which I thought was a bit overdone until I realized he had blood gushing out of his shoe. *Whew! Not shot!* Before I could get off him, I was lifted and dragged away. "Help me! Someone help me, I've been shot!!" Ritter screamed.

"Oh, shut up, Ritter," I snapped as I got to my feet. He was a disgusting maggot in my opinion and deserved everything he got.

Reed held me tightly, mumbling something about forgiveness, stupidity, and I don't know what. I pushed him away and examined at myself. My beautiful new suit was stained and wrinkled. My sexy heels were snapped at the stem. I was practically kidnapped at gunpoint, and my heart was broken all because of this man. I was royally pissed.

"It was the earrings! He bugged me!" I pointed to a crying Ritter.

"Help me! I'm bleeding to death!" Ritter yelled.

Reed tried to hold me in his arms again. "I'm so sorry, love. So very sorry."

I stumbled back, taking off my one good shoe and threw it at him, hitting him square in the chest. "You didn't believe in me. I've never given you any reason to doubt me, and yet, you believed I would...I would..." I shut up and searched for something else to throw at him.

"Could someone call an ambulance? I'm bleeding out here!"

Reed advanced, sadness in his expression with every step

he took. "I was a crazy fool, Miranda. I admit it. I love you, and to think you had betrayed me…" He swallowed hard.

"Yes, that was your first thought! Me! Not the research people, or I don't know who else, but me!" I poked him in the chest.

"Could someone help me off the ground?" Ritter whined.

"It's because I love you, woman! I was vulnerable, finally trusting, and then—"

"Well, you had better start trusting me, mister, or there is no point in continuing this relationship!" I shoved him, and he stumbled, falling on his butt for once.

"I feel weak. I don't think I can stand. Help me!"

"SHUT UP, RITTER!" Reed and I shouted in unison.

I could hear the sirens in the distance. Someone had called the cops and probably an ambulance for Ritter, not that the bastard deserved it, and only then did I notice George had his gun trained on him while Ritter's gun sat firmly under his foot.

Reed started to get up, and I glanced away. Unfortunately, I finally saw Ritter's wound, well, part of it. His shoe had a big hole where blood trickled out, but it was enough to send me over the edge. I shook in the aftermath, swaying on my feet. Reed was there immediately, holding me as I prayed my stomach wouldn't empty the donut and coffee I had consumed.

"Shh, Miranda, love, it's OK. Everyone is fine."

A large sweater was draped over my shoulders, the smell of Bengay and Avon's Timeless doing more to warm me than the wool. Agnes was here. She wouldn't let anything happen to me. I reached for her hand, feeling the arthritic fingers take hold of mine.

I was led over to an ambulance where Reed insisted I be checked over. I complied, numbly aware of questions being asked and answered by Reed and some of the witnesses. I simply wished to go home and sleep.

After what seemed like hours, I was allowed to leave. Reed stayed behind to assist the police with the investigation. Agnes drove me home, tucked me into my bed. The last thing I remember was Prince crawling onto the bed with me as Agnes snored in the nearby chair. What happened to Reed was anyone's guess.

Chapter Fourteen

I awoke slowly, the sunlight streaming across the bed, warming my body. I stretched before snuggling back under the covers for a moment, enjoying the gentle lap of the waves against the ship. Reaching out, I found the other side empty and slightly cool. Reed must have been up for a while.

Yes, I took him back. Was there ever any doubt? He was the love of my life, and he felt and acted truly remorseful. I understood how love messes with your head. Hadn't I tried to hide from him early in our relationship? Well, I wound up exposing more than just my face that time, but my heart knew it was because of love, not curiosity, that I tried to hide. Umm, well, mostly.

I grabbed a robe to cover my nightie in case others were up and about to head up the stairs to the main deck. Reed's yacht was fabulously made, room enough for parties and six bedrooms for guests, which were all occupied at the moment with my daughter and my friends, including Agnes.

I saw him standing near the bow, coffee cup in hand, contemplating the water. Before I approached him, I took a moment to sear this vision in my mind. My man. This incredibly handsome, sexy, and honorable man was mine. The fact he was ridiculously rich didn't even matter. He could be standing on a pile of coal and he'd still have a commanding presence. God, I loved him so much!

He must have heard my sigh because he turned around and opened his arms. I hurried into them, feeling safe and loved. It was my favorite way to wake up and go to sleep, with Reed Michael's arms around me.

"What would you like to do today, love? Shopping? Tours?" he asked, kissing the top of my head. "We are close to Sardinia. Maybe another two hours."

"What time is it?" I snuggled into him. He smelled of man and sleep. I sniffed again. Maybe it was weird, but I couldn't seem to get enough of him. Everything about him called to me.

"Just past seven. We could have coffee and a snack here and then head into the town for brunch if you like."

Reluctantly, I stepped away, kissing his jaw. "Whatever you think, love. I'll go and change."

"Don't go changing, I love you just the way you are." He sang out softly.

I couldn't help it, I beamed up at him. He was the sweetest man. I started sashaying back to the stairs.

"Oh, Miranda?"

"Yes?" I turned to find Reed on bended knee.

"Marry me." Those intense dark eyes shone with love and a tiny bit of worry. A velvet box sat opened in his hand, the largest diamond I had ever seen catching the morning light.

I gasped, then screamed, "Yes!!" Running at him, I didn't think about my speed or the awkward position he was trying to get up from. I launched myself at him, smothering him with my body.

Unfortunately, the angle wasn't quite right, and we toppled onto the sofa cushions. Reed flung one of his arms out to break our fall. When he did that, I watched in horror as the box and the beautiful ring took flight from his fingers and soared over the railing, landing into the water with barely a splash.

I shrieked in dismay, climbing poor Reed's body like a ladder to try and vault myself off his chest, over that same railing in an attempt to retrieve my ring.

"Are you crazy, woman?" Reed growled, hauling me back in a none-too-gentle grip.

"I lost my ring!" I wailed, flailing in his arms.

"It can be replaced. You can't, Miranda."

"But it was a Harry Winston, wasn't it?" I sobbed into my hands.

"Er, yes. But no harm done, love. I'll get you another." He hugged me.

"That's not the point!" I scowled at him then looked past him in shock.

My friends were standing there, in various states of nightwear, gaping at us. Well, all except Sadie. She was naked and staring at us.

"Sadie!" Reed turned, and I quickly covered his eyes as I yelled, "Get some clothes on!"

"Why the hell are you screeching at this ungodly hour?" Kimy grumbled between yawns.

Agnes took in the scene. "I take it she said yes?"

Reed nodded, still trying to evade my hands on his eyes. "Stop!" I scolded him.

Jerome shrugged out of his robe, eyes closed, and Tessa covered Sadie, who appeared to be insulted that her nudity caused a problem.

Agnes' words seemed to penetrate their collective brains, and as one, they converged on us with hugs, kisses, and congratulations!

"Let's see the ring!" Tessa exclaimed.

I pouted and hung my head. "I've already lost it. That was the scream. It got tossed overboard."

"Wait a minute! Didn't I hear something about Harry Winston?" Chloe asked.

Kimy blew out a shrill breath.

"Mother! You didn't!" My daughter confronted me–I hadn't noticed her come up the stairs.

I simply nodded and burst into a fresh round of tears.

Reed held me in his arms and waved the crowd back. "I told you, it's going to be fine."

I looked up, bumping his chin with my head again and scowled. "How can you say that? Some damn fish has probably swallowed my engagement ring!"

He kissed me quickly. "Did you really think I'd forgotten who I was marrying? It's fully insured. When we get to land,

I'll call the insurance company and the jeweler. He can have another one made."

Everyone started laughing except me. I still felt terrible. "Are you sure you know what you're getting yourself into?" I whispered to him.

He stopped grinning, and holding my face with both hands, he met my gaze. I saw the love shining in his eyes, telling me everything I needed to know. "I've never been more sure of anything in my life, Miranda. I can't imagine a life without you in it." He kissed me softly. "I don't even want to contemplate it."

"I love you, Reed. I've loved you for a long time. I'll always be there for you." I kissed him back.

"Eww, gross," my daughter made gagging noises, but her eyes twinkled.

Kimy and Chloe did the "aww" thing.

Jerome and Tessa disappeared—I assume back into their bedroom.

And Agnes…she simply smiled and declared, "I'm hungry. What's there to eat around this tuna boat?"

It felt amazing to be surrounded by friends on the best day of my life.

Acknowledgments

There would be no Minx without the friendship of two spectacularly courageous women - Miranda Lynn and Maria Vickers.

Miranda was brave enough to say yes to my crazy idea of a video commercial for the book. She took the time out of her own busy schedule to spend the day in crazy high heels and a floppy hat to bring Minx to life. I lost count of how many times she walked down that sidewalk and then came back to do it again. She's funny, fierce and a helluva of writer herself - check out the back of the book! So thank you, Miranda, for being there for me, encouraging me, and for simply being You. Without your help, Miranda Blake would still be struggling to get up off the ground.

My undying gratitude goes to Maria Vickers, editor, formatter, promotional guru, and also a fabulous writer in her own right. Because of a chance meeting at a book event, we became friends. I like to think God knew I needed help so he sent me an angel. Without her, I probably would have given up on Minx. Her priceless advice and support have helped me grow to be a better writer; her compassion and friendship have shown me how to be a better friend, and her courage and optimism have given me the tools I need to be a better person.

Finally, my fans and family have put up with my quirks, my fits over characters, my worry and my procrastination. Not to mention my actual falls, moonings, and the occasional sprained ankle. Thank you for always helping me up, you are my world and I love you!

EXCERPT

Noah walked into Sweetie Pie's Bakery and Cafe. His instincts had led him here. He knew another shifter was in this place. He took a sniff, letting his nose lead him to the man he had been chasing along the riverfront. He caught a whiff of perfume, saw the two women sitting near the window, drinking coffee and enjoying bearclaw pastries. He smiled slightly in their direction, but turned swiftly as the curtains parted behind the counter and his senses came alive. BEAR. He forced his jaw back where it had dropped open as the vision of beauty came closer. Platinum blonde hair piled high behind a pink bandana, voluptuous body stuffed into waitress uniform, and tall enough to see past his shoulder to the ladies near the window. She waved to the kids walking past the place. They returned the wave, and seconds later, the bell over the door rang as they bustled in. This was definitely not the intruder he had been chasing. THIS was his mate. Holy Shit! He had just found his mate!

About Maggie Adams

Maggie Adams is an Amazon Best Selling contemporary romance author. Her first book in the Tempered Steel Series, Whistlin' Dixie, debuted in Amazon's Top 100 for Women's Fiction, humor, on November, 2014 and then again at #61 in 2016. Since then, she has consistently made the Amazon best seller 5-star list with Leather and Lace, Something's Gotta Give, Love, Marriage & Mayhem, and Forged in Fire. Her series has launched the tiny town of Grafton, Illinois, into International recognition with sales in Mexico, Ireland, Scotland, Australia and the UK.

Other Books by Maggie Adams

Lustful Legacy

The Trouble with Angels

Crazy Daisy

<u>TEMPERED STEEL SERIES</u>

Whistlin' Dixie, Book One in the Tempered Steel Series

Leather and Lace, Book two

Something's Gotta Give, Book three

Getting Lucky, A Tempered Steel Novella

Love, Marriage & Mayhem, Book four

Forged in Fire, Book five

Cold as Ice, Book six

The Tempered Steel Series, Books 1-3

The Tempered Steel Series, Books 4-6

THE LUSTFUL TRILOGY

Lustful Letters

Lustful Lies

Lustful Longings

THE LEGENDS SERIES

Legends: Catori

RELEASED MARCH 2019
UNBREAK ME
(An MM Romance)

BLURB:

They were supposed to be together forever. That was the plan, but through a cruel twist of fate the night before their three-year anniversary, Tex Davis lost the one man he would ever love, Memphis King. A year has passed and he still hasn't been able to move on. Everyone tells him it's time, but what do they know? Memphis was his partner in love and life. Losing him, broke Tex.

Tex has been given an opportunity to move from New York to Seattle. His friends and family are encouraging him to take it, but he has already decided to decline the offer because that would mean leaving Memphis behind.

Then something happened.

Whether it be fate or something else, Memphis came back to him. Tex's first love is supposed to help him move on, but not even Memphis can bring himself to force Tex to let him go.

Is it so wrong to want to spend forever with the person you loved most? Both hearts are begging to be unbroken.

Tagline:
Two broken hearts, one wandering soul.

PURCHASE LINKS:
***AVAILABLE IN KU*
AMAZON US:
www.amazon.com/dp/B07MC5XWG6
AMAZON UK:
www.amazon.co.uk/dp/B07MC5XWG6
AMAZON FR:
www.amazon.fr/dp/B07MC5XWG6
AMAZON CA:
www.amazon.ca/dp/B07MC5XWG6
AMAZON AU:
www.amazon.com.au/dp/B07MC5XWG6

Goodreads:
https://www.goodreads.com/book/show/
43514149-unbreak-me

ABOUT MARIA VICKERS

Maria Vickers currently lives in St. Louis, MO with her pug, Spencer Tracy. She has always had a passion for writing and after she became disabled in 2010, she decided to use writing as her escape. She believes that life is about what you make of it. You have to live it to the fullest no matter the circumstances.

From a young age, she has always loved books and even dreamed of being an author when she was younger. Growing up in the Navy, she used to weave tales for her siblings and her friends about anything and everything. And when she wasn't creating her own stories, she had a book in her hand. They transported her to another world. She hopes that with her books, her readers have the same experience and that they can relate to her characters.

Getting sick changed her life forever, but it also opened doors for her that she thought would always be out of reach.

AUTHOR LINKS:

Newsletter:
http://eepurl.com/cvH8tX

Join her reader group, Maria's Love Seekers.
https://www.facebook.com/groups/MariaLoveSeekers/

facebook.com/mariavickersbooks

twitter.com/mvauthor

instagram.com/authormariavickers

amazon.com/author/mariavickers

bookbub.com/authors/maria-vickers

goodreads.com/mariavickers_author

CHAPTER ONE

One year. One year since Tex lost Memphis. One year since his lover had been killed, and it had yet to get easier. Everyone kept telling him it would, it never did. There were times he thought about ending it all, and then he would feel something…hear something that would make him change his mind. Actually, sometimes he thought he was losing it.

And today, he called in sick to work, unable to get out of bed until this afternoon. When he finally emerged, he only relocated to the living room after grabbing a full bottle of Southern Comfort and plopped down on the sofa. The very sofa he and Memphis picked out together. It had been their first major furniture decision when they decided to move in together. The moment the delivery men left, Tex and Memphis broke it in thoroughly, wearing themselves out.

Tex looked around the room. It seemed so empty

without Memphis, and he felt so lost without his lover. He'd been sitting here for hours? Minutes? It had to be some amount of time since the bottle was half gone, and he was feeling a drunken morose engulfing him. He could not stop the bitter question from leaving his lips, the very question he had been asking daily since losing his best friend, lover, other half…his everything. "Why? Why Memphis? Why did you have to go? Why did it have to be you and not me?"

Shaking his head, Tex sniffled and brought his glass filled with amber liquid to his lips. "When you left, it completely broke my heart…I'm still broken. I need to hear you say that you love me one more time. A million more times, but that won't happen. Can't happen." He took another gulp, draining the glass before wiping his nose with the back of his hand.

More tears were falling, but he ignored them like he'd done every time they sprang up. It was easy to do after all this time; besides, they didn't matter. Nothing mattered any longer and hadn't for a year.

He sobbed again and then got angry. "I wish you could come back to fix me, fix what you destroyed when you left, but that's a pipe dream. You got mad, said your peace, and then stormed out of here. If you had just waited…" Tex choked on his words.

Pouring himself another glassful of liquor, he breathed out as drops of saltwater fell on his coffee table. He should probably stop drinking and put himself to bed to finish wallowing there, but he couldn't. It had been one year. One year since that fateful night…unlucky night more like it. One year since he'd heard Memphis' voice, touched his body, and the loss Tex felt that night remained just as acute tonight as it did then. He thought time was supposed to heal the wounds, to lessen the pain…lies. All lies. "It's my fault, Memphis. If I hadn't been spiteful and allowed that monstrous bitch, jealousy, to cloud my judgment…if only. If only. I regretted everything, regretted that the last words I spoke to you were bitter and vile. I can't forget you, can't move on. I'm lonely without you, Memphis. It hurts so much that you aren't here." He wailed like a banshee, his cry full of sorrow and pain.

Tex downed the entire glass, hoping that the pain would deaden, or that he would stop feeling anything. Maybe if he drank enough, he could join Memphis.

Grabbing a pillow from the couch, Tex threw it across the room where it bounced off the window overlooking the streets of Manhattan. "You were supposed to go right! You were supposed to go to Christy's apartment!" He wailed, "Why weren't you at your sister's? Why did you have to go the other way? She looked horrible because she had been sick, even her blue hair looked green." Tex snorted mirthlessly.

"You went the other way. Why? Why the other way? Was it because of the bar? The one where we met? Memphis, do you remember? I was sitting at the bar, and you walked up to me and gave me that stupid, cheesy pickup line, 'I seem to have lost my phone number, can I have yours?' So stupid. I remember I said, 'That's a shame because I lost mine too. I guess we're both screwed.' You winked at me then. I should have known something bad was going to come out of your mouth…your sexy mouth. 'Not

167

yet, but we could be.' I laughed. You were always good at making me laugh, making me smile." Shaking his head and snickering, he poured another glass. If he destroyed his liver, if he got alcohol poisoning, then maybe he could be with Memphis again.

"There has always only been you. You got me when no one else did. You loved me…I loved you. Three years. We were together one night shy of three years. We never got to see four." Tex fell back and stared up at the blue ceiling with white fluffy clouds painted on it, his tears falling down his face like two rivers. There was no point in wiping them away because there was no end to them, and he couldn't staunch them even if he tried. Memphis was gone and would forever remain gone.

It had been a year, and Tex floated through life, unable to move on. "I know I should continue to live for us…for you, but I don't know how," Tex's words ended on a shout, full of rage, and his face was red from more than just the alcohol.

Sitting up, Tex grabbed the bottle of Southern Comfort and raised it into the air, choosing to do away with the glass. "A toast to you and your lost life. Memphis, I still love you, and I wish every single god damned day that you were still here beside me. Each day that passes reminds me that you will never be part of my life again, that you will never hold me, never tease me again. You were funny, caring, sexy, and all mine. Forgive me…God, please forgive me for that night, for accusing you of cheating. I know you loved me. Jealousy is a fucking bitch. Somehow, I'd gotten it into my head that you were leaving me when you weren't. I found out after.

Sometimes I think I killed you. I'm sorry. So, so sorry." He whimpered as he took in a shaky breath. "Memphis, I will always love you and only you."

He chugged the rest of the amber liquid from the bottle and fell to his side onto the couch, resting his head on the cushion. More tears fell. They never stopped. Even if they weren't falling down his face, his soul cried and mourned the loss of his friend and lover. The pain hadn't stopped since the day he lost Memphis.

I wish you were here to fix the heart you broke when you died, Memphis, Tex thought to himself as he closed his eyes. Before he fully submitted to the effects of the alcohol though, he felt a set of lips press against his. "Memphis, love…" he slurred, his words tapering off as he finally allowed himself to completely fall into the void.

NEW RELEASE
Jerome: Pack Alpha

An alpha who has to think outside of the box.
In order to secure his pack's survival.
Because every shifter species is in jeopardy.

Jerome has a plan that he knows will work.
Convincing the rest of the supernatural world is the next
step.
Sterling has always supported Jerome's vision and travels
with him to help him convince the council.

His job is to also make sure he comes out of that meeting

alive. What they come home to will change Jerome's world for good.

ABOUT MIRANDA LYNN

Time Travel and Paranormal Romance author who helps you escape reality one book at a time.

Miranda is a mother to two teenage boys who are sure they know it all, two four-legged fur babies on who believes she is a lap dog at 75lb and one who takes over pillows at night and is smallish at 15lb. She is thankful her husband doesn't mind the extra voices in her head and her constant talking to them.

Miranda is an only child who grew up on a dairy farm in Illinois which left her plenty of time to make up stories in her head for entertainment. She currently resides in Tennessee where she wonders if Mother Nature will ever stop with the hormonal mood swings. She fuels herself with coffee, chocolate, and wine.

AUTHOR LINKS:

Website
www.mirandalynn.com

Street Team

https://www.facebook.com/groups/367841766921211

Newsletter

https://www.subscribepage.com/MirandaLynnsMusings

facebook.com/MirandaLynnBks

twitter.com/MirandaLynnBks

instagram.com/authormirandalynn

goodreads.com/Miranda_Lynn

amazon.com/author/miranda-lynn

www.ingramcontent.com/pod-product-compliance
Lightning Source LLC
Chambersburg PA
CBHW070031120726
47909CB00003B/1128